The Rose and the Lion

A Novel

Charles J. Musser

Based on the life and times of Richard Pierpoint

Also by Charles J. Musser

Gichi Manidoo

Cover artwork
By Alex Nery

Charcoal drawing *Shenandoah*
By Yessika Figueira

Beneath the palm-trees on the plain
Once more a king he strode

—Longfellow

The Rose and the Lion

The Rose and the Lion

The Rose and the Lion

Chapter 1

Connecticut 1775

The fruity, warm scent of honeysuckle wafted in the air as Richard strolled down a narrow path in the Shetucket Woods. Two dragonflies hovered around his head, circled, and shot away like arrows with a faint buzzing sound. He froze.

A young woman stood slightly off the path with her back to him. She was wearing a simple, unadorned yellow dress and a white bonnet. She held a witch-hazel dowsing stick as she walked forward through a small patch of wild clover speckled with purple blossoms. The dark brown skin of her hands contrasted with the garment, and her face, at least the part of it he could see, was smooth with strong cheekbones and a full mouth.

The woods were far from town, and few people ever came here. He had never seen her before. He had come because it was his favorite place to meditate. Often, when the mood befell him, he would sing some of the many songs he carried in his head. The quiet, the privacy, the smells and sights, were intoxicating to him. Solitude was a commodity he held very dear.

He glanced down at his palms and flipped his hand over. Her skin color was darker than his. He was sure she was a house slave, judging from her clothing and bearing. She stood tall and straight. He'd seen so many men and women bent by the unyielding toil of the fields, their spirit broken by the bitter stinging of the lash.

Why was she dowsing here, of all places? He almost called out to her, then caught himself. She appeared to be in a trance, not watching where each step took her as she followed the bobbing tip of the dowsing rod.

He crouched on one knee. She turned and looked about. *Was she startled?* She looked in his direction. *Had she seen him?* She turned away, but he had gotten a clear view of her face. It was difficult for him to get a breath of air. All he cared about was holding on to the image in his mind of her face looking over her shoulder at him. Her eyes flashed, her full lips pressed together above a slightly dimpled chin. He was suddenly warm.

He loosened his tunic, removed his cap, and stuffed it in his breeches' pocket. He stood again and watched her. Her gestures were smooth and fluid, like a dancer's, each one deliberate and carefully placed. He took two steps toward her, careful not to make a sound. She whipped her head to the side and faced him.

She spoke just loud enough for him to hear her between her clenched teeth.

"Git. These woods mine."

Richard stood taller, and raised his chin. His muscles tensed, and warmth crept up the back of his neck. He scowled. These were his woods, not hers. How dare she claim them and ruin his meditating?

He opened his mouth to chastise her, as she deserved, but then noticed the tip of her dowsing rod began to tug downward. She slowed and then stopped, setting it quietly on the ground beside her. She removed her bonnet and tucked it into the neckline of her blouse. Her hair was bound tight to her head by a white cloth band which she untied at the back, freeing her black curls. They uncoiled and bobbed about her face and neck. She pulled the hem of her skirt up and folded it into a thin cotton belt around her waist, exposing her legs to just above the knees. She hesitated, like a pause in a melody.

Richard held his breath.

She lunged toward a small patch of rough, prickly shrub. A gray hare flew out the other side, just beyond the tips of her fingers, and bounded away. She let out a cry, and was after it immediately.

The hare jerked its body to the left and careened down a steep hill. It circled back toward him. *She's lost it,* Richard knew. He sneered at her bumbling, but the sneer faded when she made a giant leap and was behind it again, now closer than ever. He'd never seen a woman move so quickly. He shook his head to clear the shock. *Never seen anyone move like that.*

He jumped over a mossy boulder, intending to cut off the animal and help her, but at the last second, it scuttled close to the ground and shot between his legs, then hopped over the boulder behind him. She flew by Richard, her skirt brushing his thigh.

She yelled at him, "Fool!"

Fool, indeed! Fists clenched, Richard chased after the woman and the hare.

They tore through brambles and wild raspberry bushes, and the thorns snagged their clothes. They bounded over a wide but shallow stream that splashed their thighs with cold water. Through blue spruce and white birch, they dodged and twisted, following the darting animal.

A low-hanging branch banged against his forehead, sending him sprawling, and he tumbled down a small hill into black and sulfurous swamp muck.

He wrinkled his nose and groaned. The muck rose to mid-shin and he grabbed a nearby branch to pull himself up onto the dry bank, his face covered with the sloppy and stinky mud.

He lay on his back and watched white clouds scud by overhead between the tall trees. A droplet of mud seeped into the corner of his mouth. It tasted putrid and sour. *Damn that woman!*

He continued to stare upwards and heard footsteps. From the corner of his eye, the hare appeared already field-dressed, hanging upside down a foot or so above his head. He rubbed his eyes. They stung and burned. That damn woman stood over him and dangled the dead animal. One hand held its hind legs, her other hand on her hip. She had raised an eyebrow, and her ebony skin glistened with perspiration in the dappled light.

He reached for the hare and she yanked it away. He sighed and sat up.

She tucked the carcass in her belt and rolled down the hem of her skirt. A slight smile broke at the corner of her mouth.

She held out her hand. "Shenandoah," she said. "You stink."

He couldn't stifle the chuckle that rose in his throat. He stood and shook her hand.

"Richard."

"Uh huh. You always that clumsy?" she asked, handing him the white headband that she pulled from her belt. He took it and shook his head, then used it to wipe the muck from his face. He held it back out to her.

She laughed and shrugged. "Don't want it now, fool."

"Why you calling me fool?"

"Everyone a fool to me until they prove otherwise."

"Well, these woods are my woods, you hear? Chase your hare in some other woods."

She turned and walked away.

"Hey," he yelled. "You hear me?"

She kept walking. "Damn woman," he said under his breath. He waited to see if she had heard him.

Stopping, she pulled her bonnet out demurely from her blouse neckline and tied it on. She turned and looked at him. Picking up her dowsing rod, she pointed it at him and shook it.

"You don't own these woods, Richard."

"Neither do you, Shenandoah. Don't you tell me to git."

She smiled. "All right, maybe you ain't a fool. Any man or woman thinks they own the ground and the rivers and the trees and animals may be crazy, but they ain't no fools. They're dreamers," she said and winked.

Richard laughed. "Best kind of crazy."

She nodded and once again walked away.

He cupped his hands and yelled at her back. "Who the hell dowses for hares?" When she didn't answer, he added, "You coming back here tomorrow?"

Her laughter echoed in the tall trees.

Chapter 2

Connecticut 1776

R ichard Pierpoint, thirty-one years old, stood at the edge of a market and surveyed the crowd. Vendors hawked vegetables, chickens, fish, pottery, and various other sundries.

Being a house slave, he was dressed in comfortable trousers and a white blouse. Over his shoulder he carried two empty sacks. He glanced to one side of the square, where a hangman's scaffold stood.

Two men approached with a chained prisoner between them. One was a hangman, a burly chap with thick forearms. He wore a mask, as prescribed by law, but everyone knew he was the blacksmith, Jimmy Lancaster. The other man was the county sheriff, Fergus Shoal, a former minister who had been defrocked after fornicating with another man's wife behind the altar. Apparently, this was just the sort of behavior that recommended him as a sheriff to the voters, who elected him within a month despite his indiscretions.

The prisoner was a Black slave, about fifty years old, named William Smith. His face was swollen, bloody, and battered. Eyes downcast, he was calm and resolved, his hands tied behind him.

Richard knew that Smith had been tried and convicted for ferrying stolen weapons, including British muskets, across state lines from New York in a barge. Allegedly, they were to be delivered to various rebellious Negroes. He also faced charges for resisting arrest—slapping Sheriff Shoal in the face with an odorous dead mackerel—and planning to murder everyone in the Connecticut delegation to the Continental Congress, a prodigious feat if it had been accomplished. The trial had lasted one hour.

Richard scanned the rest of the market carefully, and his eyes landed on Shenandoah examining some items from a cloth vendor on the other side of the square.

Their eyes met, and she nodded to him. She wore a calico dress with a fitted bodice that closed in the front. She smiled briefly. Richard returned the smile and nodded.

A small crowd gathered at the base of the scaffold. The prisoner, the hangman, and the sheriff, mounted the short staircase. The slaves in attendance kept their eyes down and avoided looking directly, stealing furtive glances at the spectacle.

Captain Lucius Prescott, Richard's owner, walked up behind him, catching Richard watching the scaffold. Prescott wore the uniform and rank of a captain in the American Continental Army. He was an angular, lanky man with a strong jaw and bushy eyebrows.

"Enjoying the entertainment, are we?" Prescott said to him.

Richard regarded his own unpolished leather boots.

Prescott chuckled. They stood in front of a pottery vendor's table. Above the table, a sign read "Authentic Staffordshire Pottery." A young Black boy carried new vases from a cart and set them on the counter. Richard smiled at him.

Prescott picked up a particularly garish vase, examined it, and snapped a riding crop he carried in his other hand against his thigh.

"Trash," Prescott said to the disheveled man who was

wearing a black cowl and missing all of his upper and lower front teeth. "It's as certain this was imported from England as your sniveling smile is sincere." He tossed the vase roughly back on the table.

"Is that an insult, sir?" hissed the vendor through the gap in his mouth.

"You're aware that non-English imports are prohibited," Prescott continued, ignoring the question. He turned to Richard, "Quit dallying, boy, and get the goddamned potatoes. Try to ensure they aren't rotten this time, if it isn't too much trouble for you. I'm going home."

"Yes, Master Prescott."

Richard made his way to the vegetable section of the market. He once again searched for Shenandoah. He couldn't find her. She never seemed to stay in one place more than a few seconds, and flitted about like a butterfly. *Settle down, woman*, he thought ruefully.

Isaac Whiles, a slave in his late sixties, sold potatoes behind a pine stall. Isaac was short, but carried himself with a regal bearing. He usually spoke with a deep resonance that made you listen to every word, as if some deity had come to earth to impart wisdom to mere mortals. The reverie was spoiled, however, when he cursed, which was often, for his voice would rise several octaves. It was unnerving, Richard had long ago decided.

Richard walked up, and the two nodded in acknowledgment. From the scaffold, a voice rang out. Everyone in the square stopped, and they stared at the three men atop it. The sheriff read from a scroll in a piercing, high voice. He held it out as far as his hands could reach, his back arched and head bent back, as if he were reading it to the sky.

"Slave William Smith, having been found guilty of rebellion and conspiring to cause rebellion and malicious and nefarious intrigue among the peaceful Negroes of this colony, you are sentenced to hang by the neck until you be dead. Have you any final words?"

The condemned man raised his eyes, straightened himself, and stared directly ahead. "I did nothing wrong, and the Lord God Almighty knows that. I proved that I'm a man. Until the last man's free, ain't nobody free." He turned and addressed the hangman. "Get it done."

The hangman yanked a hood over Smith's head and placed the rope around his neck. Now many of the slaves in the square turned away, nervously pretending everything was normal and they could return to business as usual.

The sheriff nodded to the hangman, who pulled a lever that opened the trapdoor beneath Smith's feet.

As Smith fell, there was a *crash* just behind Richard. He swung around to see the young boy from the pottery vendor with a shattered vase at his feet. The boy froze as he realized what he'd done, and Richard stepped toward him as the rest of the crowd watched Smith's lifeless body sway.

The boy looked up at Richard, then glanced toward the pottery vendor, who had not yet noticed the boy's mistake. He shook, terror in his eyes.

Richard bent down, picked up the pieces of the broken vase, placed them in one of his empty bags, and took out a silk purse.

"How much?" he asked the shaking boy.

"It's...it's broke."

"How much if it wasn't broke?"

The boy understood what Richard was up to and turned away in embarrassment. Richard pulled out three coins from his purse and held them out to the boy, wary of the vendor who now made his way toward them.

"You take this now, you hear me?"

The boy still refused the coins.

As the vendor came up, the boy reluctantly held out his hand, and Richard dropped the coins into his palm. The vendor grabbed the boy's wrist and twisted. The boy opened his hand, revealing the coins, which the vendor snatched in haste. He examined them closely.

"My master realized his mistake and sent me to purchase one of your fine imported English vases, sir."

"Did he now?" The vendor's eyes narrowed. He stared at Richard's bag, then examined the coins in his hand. He nearly said something but changed his mind.

"Next time you buy them from me, not my boy, you hear?" A slender rope of tobacco spit dangled from his toothless mouth.

"Yes, sir." Richard winked at the boy when he was sure the vendor wasn't watching and walked away toward Isaac's vegetable stand.

He looked around the square, but there was still no sign of Shenandoah. He took a deep breath and exhaled. She made his heart beat fast when she was near, but he was damned if he liked being in the thrall of such feelings.

A man should be in control, right? He chuckled. *We like to think we are around women.*

Isaac finished with a customer as Richard walked up.

"Thank you, missus. Isaac do appreciate it." As the woman left with a small sack of carrots, Richard tossed his remaining empty sack on the counter. Without looking up, Isaac began to fill the sack with potatoes from a bushel.

"He's wise to it. I need good ones this time," Richard said.

Isaac stopped, glanced back, and chuckled. He dumped the rotten potatoes back into the bushel and started to fill the bag with good potatoes from a large bin. He set it back on the counter. As he did so, both men turned and watched William Smith's body being cut down and placed in a cart.

"Did he talk?" Richard asked quietly.

"You mean did he give up our names?"

"That's what I mean."

"What do you think?"

Richard looked deeply into Isaac's eyes. "He was a brave man."

"That he was, brother." Isaac held out his hand. "Same as usual."

"No money today. Bought me a vase."

"I saw." Isaac grinned. "Well, the money you and I made this year on those rotten potatoes more than covers it. These are on the house."

The two men shook hands.

As he turned away, his eyes met Shenandoah's. She was about twenty yards away, carrying a small sack of newly purchased linens. His heart raced and he heard it in his ears. They moved toward each other, but before they could take more than a few steps, the thump and whistle of a drum and fife came from the edge of the market.

Around the corner of an alley marched four British soldiers in uniform, two with muskets, and two with the musical instruments, followed by an officer. They stopped, and the officer nailed a bill to a post. He unrolled a copy, cleared his throat, and began to read in a booming voice.

"By His Excellency the Right Honorable John Earl of Dunmore, His Majesty's Lieutenant and Governor-General of the Colony and Vice-Admiral of the fame."

Hisses and catcalls came from the crowd.

"I do hereby declare all indentured servants, Negroes, or others enslaved, free that are able and willing to bear arms, they joining his Majesty's troops as soon as may be, for the more speedily reducing this Colony to a proper sense of their duty, to his Majesty's crown and dignity."

Boos rumbled like thunder.

"God save the king!" yelled the officer.

"Go to hell! Damn your king!" The crowd closed in.

The British soldiers slowly backed up, muskets raised, bayonets affixed. As they retreated into the alley and disappeared, a man tore the bill from the post and ripped it to shreds. Another man climbed the scaffold and yelled to the milling horde.

"They tax us without representation. And now they try to take our property, our means of life, away from us. These are devils, not men. They corrupt our Negroes and tempt them into murdering us in our beds as we sleep."

The crowd wailed, raised their fists, and threw rotten fruit and vegetables toward the alley where the British had retreated.

Richard motioned over his shoulder to Shenandoah.

She nodded, and they both moved through the throng to a street that ran toward the town's brothels and taverns. As they rounded the corner, together at last, their hands touched briefly. The tight curls of her hair bounced as she shook her head, the twist of a grin at her lips.

He wanted to hold her hand, to feel her warm skin. It had been nearly a year since he first met her in the Shetucket Woods and they'd grown closer, but always surreptitiously, carefully. Unapproved liaisons between slaves were a dangerous endeavor.

They walked in silence beside each other, stealing glances. Every time Richard saw her up close, he was struck by how beautiful she was. Even the idealized version of her he kept in his mind couldn't do justice to the graceful beauty she wore in real life, like the morning wears a robin's song.

Her hair hung in coils, and her lips were full. Her eyes appeared to be cut from gems: brown, lustrous and infused with living fire. He knew her gentle and sinuous movement through the world was only the front of a tossed coin, apparently spinning constantly. The back of the coin was an easily triggered temper, a sharp tongue, and an unshakeable judgment that tolerated little supplication.

He sighed. *I'm no poet, I'm a fighter. Leave the poetry to dreamers.*

His sigh brought a quick glance from Shenandoah as they walked.

"You okay?" she asked.

He nodded and took her hand as they veered between two small buildings and followed a narrow road that led into the forest. Ahead of them were several other slaves. He glanced behind and saw four more following them. They rounded a bend and came to an open field through which a small river flowed. Next to the river sat a brick and mortar building with animal skins hung on racks beside the water. It was the town tannery, and the stench was overwhelming as they got closer, a mixture of abrasive nostril-burning chemicals with rotting flesh and feces. Richard clenched his teeth and Shenandoah covered her face with her inner elbow.

Guarding the door to the building stood a field slave dressed in dirty osnaburg breeches and a sweaty shirt, his massive arms folded. He surveyed the approaching groups of people with a sullen stare. He ignored Richard and Shenandoah as they passed him and entered.

The inside was gloomy. Large wooden vats sat in the corners with various animal hides piled around the imposing room. Filled with Black men and women who talked in tight groups, they milled about, their conversations animated and punctuated with laughter. Richard coughed deeply and wrinkled his nose. He wasn't quite used to the smell yet. The stench, and distance from town, made this the perfect meeting place since it was run during the day by slaves.

Men and women swore, sweated, spat on the floor, told stories that ended with belly laughs and thighs being slapped, each emotion exaggerated. For a brief time, they were free—free from being observed, judged, hated, maligned, belittled. Contributing even more to the sense of freedom and exhilaration was the knowledge that what they were doing was dangerous and prohibited.

Richard and Shenandoah moved to the wall and sat on the floor. Isaac entered, noticed them and walked up. He nodded to Richard and tipped his hat to Shenandoah.

"Ma'am."

Shenandoah smiled at him. She reached up to her thigh under her skirt and pulled out a knife with a six-inch blade. Picking up a stick on the floor beside her, she casually began to whittle. Isaac whistled, shook his head, and looked to Richard, who shrugged.

"Women got plenty of surprises under their skirts," Isaac said.

"So it appears," agreed Richard.

Only once had he gotten his hand under her skirt. She'd pushed it away fairly quickly, her eyes flashing at him. They had been behind a stall near the quay. There weren't many people around, but still, it had been dangerous. She'd hesitated, waited for his fingers to slide under the lower band of her shift and up—

"That'll get you worse than the lash if you get caught with it, you know," said Isaac to Shenandoah.

She continued to whittle, ignoring them both.

Slaves streamed into the building, now nearly packed. At the front was a raised dais. A frail man they knew as Quarko stepped up and surveyed the room. Quarko was the oldest known slave in the Colony of Connecticut and had been born in this land. His back was bent and his hands clubbed. He cleared his throat as the crowd moved in closer around him and grew silent.

Shenandoah and Richard stood up next to Isaac to get a better view. Shenandoah stopped whittling and pointed with the tip of her knife at the excited crowd.

"Look at 'em. They think they going home," she said.

"I don't trust the English king," said Isaac.

From the dais, Quarko's voice split the air, high and piercing. "We got us a visitor," he said and pointed to the door.

From the edge of the crowd came a booming voice.

"I speak for the king. Fight, and you will have your freedom!" said an English officer as he bounded up on the dais. Richard knew he was an officer by the fine cut and stitch of his coat and trousers but had never seen the green, rustic uniform before.

"This man is Captain Walter Butler of Butler's Rangers. I know his father, Colonel John Butler, who's a decent and fair man. All y'all listen to him with respect," said Quarko stepping back.

"I have come to tell you that the King of England begs for your help!" said Butler, stepping forward. There were widespread grunts and skeptical shaking of heads. "It's true. He doesn't know you. In fact, he doesn't care about your freedom. But he does care about winning this war with the upstart traitors. Unlike those who even now rebel against their king and country, I shall not cloak my words in hypocrisy and lies about equality and freedom. This is a business deal, nothing more."

There were nods of agreement and approval.

"Them's fancy words," yelled Isaac.

"I promise you this: inordinate hardship, likely injury, and possible death. Those aren't fancy words, those are true words and you all know it. But hardship is no stranger to the faces I see here. Every man, woman, and child has borne the lash and the shackle, endured more—suffered more— than I can dream of. But I also promise you, by my living king and God, that if you fight with us we will give you land to begin a new life, a life without the harsh and brooding shadow of a master. And most precious of all, I promise you your freedom!"

Cheers came from the crowd. Richard and Isaac stood with arms folded, nodding. There was a loud *snap* behind them. They turned to look. The branch Shenandoah had been whittling had snapped in half.

"Guess I need me a sharper knife," she said.

Isaac nodded, his eyes focused, and walked toward the crowd milling around Colonel Butler.

"We go tomorrow," Richard said as he took and squeezed her hand. "Noon. Shetucket Woods."

She nodded. "Sometimes I think maybe hope ain't so bad after all."

Chapter 3
The Way To Get There

R ichard sat cross-legged on the floor of a large kitchen in the late morning, peeling potatoes, his back bent. An iron stove behind him warmed his back. A window above a cupboard across from him let in enough light for him to see what he was doing. Prescott entered, his riding crop in his right hand, and he repeatedly slapped it against his thigh.

"Have you seen my hunting boots?"

"Under your bed, master."

"When you're done with that, gather up my hunting gear."

"I was just going to market again. We need sugar and lard."

"Do as you're told, boy. That can wait. I heard there's a nide of pheasants out by the Shetucket Creek."

"Better hunting later in the evening?"

Prescott ground his teeth. The crop *slap, slap, slapped* against his leg. Carefully, he placed his toe under the lip of the pan of peeled potatoes floating in water in front of Richard and tipped it over.

"Clean up that mess, and get ready."

"Yes, master."

****

Richard followed Prescott down a path overgrown with sumac on both sides. It ran through a meadow framed by deep forest. Prescott had changed into his Continental Army uniform.

Richard carried two Brown Bess muskets, one slung over each shoulder.

Prescott stopped and pulled a flask of whiskey from his back pocket. He drank from it, returned it to his pocket, and reached back toward Richard with an empty hand, not bothering to look. Richard handed him one of the muskets.

Prescott took aim and fired. Thirty yards away, a pheasant exploded from tall grass and flew into the air. Prescott shoved the used musket back at Richard, who quickly handed him a second one. He took aim but was too late; the pheasant was far out of range by now.

Richard reloaded the first spent musket as Prescott handed him the second.

"Not enough powder. I warned you about this."

"Yes, master."

"Useless," Prescott said. His riding crop appeared. *Slap. Slap. Slap.*

They crossed the meadow and entered the woods. The path through tall pines and oak trees crested on a small hill. Prescott sat beneath the shade of a giant oak with his flask and drank.

Richard thought he saw movement behind a dense thicket of brambles about thirty feet away, and averted his gaze. Prescott stared at Richard, who knelt on one knee, and rested the muskets on the ground, barrels pointed to the sky.

"How the hell do you stand it?" Prescott sneered.

Richard stared at him, unflinching.

"*Richard.* It's not your name. That was your first owner's name." Prescott stood, his back to the tree, downing more of the whisky. "What's your real name? You don't remember anything about it, do you?"

Richard flinched and looked away as Prescott coughed and hacked. Unbidden, Richard's dream came to him as his eyes unfocused. This was the first time while awake. He felt the ground beneath him tremble.

In his mind, a lion loped in slow motion toward him. Its head was held low, its lips curled up to expose yellowed fangs. The stomach swung from side to side as each massive paw thumped on the ground, raising a cloud of dust.

Then a woman's face, his mother's face, laughing with love, her eyes wide, hovered above him through churning dark water. He was struggling for breath, terrified of drowning. Distorted by the waves, her face dissolved, then reformed again. His ears rang, yet still he could hear the lion's growl through the water as it got closer. His mother plunged her hands into the water for him, the tips of her long fingers growing closer and closer.

She spoke his name, his *real* name. *Akachi*. His mother was the last person to ever speak it, and the sound of the word yanked like a chain on his stomach. His chest heaved, and the pressure to breathe in anything, even if it was water and thus death, became unbearable.

The memories receded, and he refocused his eyes on the thicket. A woman's head popped up. Shenandoah. He shook his head. She nodded and dropped back down.

Prescott tipped his flask upside down, shook it, and then flung it into the bushes. "You're half monkeys, half donkeys, the lot of you. Fat and lazy in your African paradise," he slurred. "While over here, corpulent King Georgie strangles us with a noose, and then—" He smacked his crop on his thigh.

"—just like that, across the deep-blue sea on a great adventure you come sailing, learn manners, learn to read and write." Prescott emptied the flask into his throat. "Are you listening to me, boy?"

"I'm listening," Richard replied, a deep resonance creeping into his voice. He stared straight into Prescott's bloodshot eyes. His master stood shakily, advanced, and circled Richard. His riding crop sliced through the air.

"See, I know you've heard all about the great Lord Dunmore and his silly proclamation, haven't you? 'Come fight against the rebels, and we'll give you freedom and land.' Tell me that all you little pikaninnies haven't heard about it."

"I've heard about it."

"You think the British give a damn about you?" Prescott's crop slapped the back of Richard's head. Richard clenched his teeth and ground his jaw.

"You want me to say what I think," Richard said slowly, more a statement than a question.

"Oh, by all means, speak freely Richard Pierpoint, Emptier of Chamber Pots. Lend me your thoughts and expound on this great matter."

"I think they know they're going to lose this war unless they can find more bodies to fight for them. I think you know, for all your fancy speeches about freedom for all men and women, that you've got no intention of granting any freedom to half a million Negro men and women living among you. Scares you, don't it?"

Prescott stopped circling behind Richard and paused. Richard heard the buzzing of grasshoppers. He could almost feel the heat of the rage emanating from his master.

"I always seem to underestimate you," Prescott sneered.

The snap of a branch came from the bushes. Prescott jerked his head and grabbed one of the loaded muskets.

"Come out, little pheasant." Prescott walked, shakily, toward the brambles.

"Ain't nuthin' there, massah," Richard said with a hitch in his voice. He knew to fall into the colloquial slave-speak when he needed something from Prescott.

Prescott raised the rifle to his shoulder. "You have one chance. Come out or die."

Shenandoah emerged from behind the bushes. She wore tight deerskin trousers and a man's purple blouse, and carried two knapsacks. Her hunting knife was strapped to her thigh in a sheath.

"See? Just a runaway." Richard took a step toward the other loaded musket on the ground.

"Well, well, well…" Prescott grinned. "You know her, don't you?"

"She's new. Can't even speak much English yet. She run away two days ago before last week's auction. Ain't nothing but a skinny little girl."

Prescott swung the rifle around and pointed it at Richard.

"You're a liar. Lewis Vern and his wife own her. You've been hiding her out here, haven't you? You sly son of a bitch."

"She ain't worth no trouble. She's leaving now, I promise."

"Purty thing, you," Prescott called to Shenandoah over his shoulder. "Come over here and stand by me. Let me see what you got under that blouse."

"You know that ain't right," Richard said. He gripped his fists tightly, then relaxed, then gripped them again.

"What I know is, you two were planning on running and being goddamn emancipated." Prescott staggered a bit, then righted himself. "So how about I save you the trouble and emancipate you both from your earthly chains?" Prescott cocked the hammer. He was about forty feet from Richard.

"Now, Captain Prescott—ain't like killing a White man, but you can still go to jail for killing a Black man, even if you own him."

"I'll take that chance. See, I knew you're planning on running away to fight for the Limeys. I own you, boy."

"I got a confession, massah," Richard said slowly. He knew he was taking a chance if he provoked Prescott, but he couldn't help himself.

"Tell me."

"Every morning when I empty your chamber pot, I save just a little bit, and then I mix it in, nice and smooth, with your dinner stew each night. That's why you been shitting brown water like a goose for the past year."

Prescott froze. Purple rage danced on his drunken face, his eyebrows and nose squished together, his lips quivered, and a thin line of spittle ran down his chin. He began to shake, and the muzzle of the musket wove back and forth. *Boom!* It fired and went high over Richard's head. Shenandoah screamed.

Enraged, Prescott threw the empty musket to the ground. His eyes settled on the remaining loaded musket at Richard's feet. Richard looked down at the weapon as well.

"Now you give me that, boy. Slave pick up a weapon, he's gonna hang."

Richard picked up the musket casually and laid it in the crook of his arm. He knew the moment had come to make the choice, to pull the trigger on his and Shenandoah's plan to run north and join the Rangers. He took a deep breath. Prescott weaved and staggered toward him, then lunged at him. Richard easily sidestepped and watched Prescott career onto his face in the dirt.

He thought about raising the musket, pointing it at him, but it felt heavy in his hand, like the time he'd been told by Prescott to kill a puppy that had wandered into the yard. He simply couldn't bring himself to do it, had lied to Prescott about it. Prescott pulled himself up on his hands and knees, trying to stand up straight, but began to puke.

Shenandoah strode up to Prescott, and stepped over him. She pulled the knife from its sheath, grabbed Prescott by his hair and yanked his head back. She put the knife to his throat and looked up at Richard, an eyebrow raised. Her hand was steady as a rock, her eyes were narrowed, centered on Richard completely. Her breath puffed out in punctuated chuffs. Prescott stared skyward, mumbling, seemingly unaware of the mortal peril he was in.

Richard shook his head. She shrugged, stepped back, and sheathed her knife. Prescott collapsed on his stomach, writhing. Richard dropped to one knee next to Prescott.

"Guess you won't be underestimating me no more, Captain."

"Go to hell."

Richard reached down, pulled the riding crop stuck in the lip of Prescott's boot, tapped him twice on the head with it, snapped it in half, and tossed it over him.

"You should have killed me. I'm going to find you," growled Prescott.

Richard leaned in close to Prescott's face.

"Us slaves take our master's names. Think I'm going be a captain. 'Captain Dick.' I like the sound of that. What you think, Captain Prescott?"

"You're a dead man."

"Ain't nobody get out of this world alive."

****

As the sun moved the late afternoon shadows across the landscape, Prescott sat tied to a large oak tree, his shoulders and abdomen secured tightly with rope. His head lolled to the side, vomit caked on his shoulder. About twenty yards away, Richard and Shenandoah sat on a fallen log, facing each other. From one of the knapsacks, Richard removed a frayed, tea-stained map and spread it carefully on the log between them. Shenandoah pointed.

"Yes, northwest. New York frontier, the Mohawk Valley." Richard spoke in a low voice so that Prescott, who was recovering from his drunken stupor, couldn't hear them.

Shenandoah picked up her knapsack and slung it, while Richard gathered up the muskets. They returned to the map that still lay on top of the log and, just as Richard was about to roll it, Shenandoah placed her finger on it and moved it to the right-hand farthest edge of the map.

"The ocean, and...?"

She moved her finger past the outer edge of the map far down the log and stopped. He looked at her and put his hand on her shoulder.

"Home. The way to get there is that way," he said, pointing. She nodded and glanced back at Prescott. "When he sobers up, he'll get loose," he continued. "But we'll be gone by then."

"Are you sure, Richard?" asked Shenandoah.

"No. But I ain't gonna kill if I don't have to kill. That's not the way to start this."

She pondered on his words, then smiled and kissed him on the lips. His eyes grew wide. He reached for her, but she laughed, pulled away, and began to jog toward the Mohawk Valley. He grabbed the muskets and ran after her.

Another memory returned as he ran, of being a boy on the African savannah, the feel of the ground under the soles of his naked feet, the satisfying slap and puff of dust, the feeling that he could run forever.

As he caught up with her, both of them turned to look back. A fat pheasant strutted a few feet in front of Prescott, and then waddled into the bushes.

Chapter 4

Butler

Captain Walter Butler of His Majesty's Rangers rode north in the early afternoon, accompanied by Eli Everly, a young lad of about twenty years who served as his aide.

Everly was a small man with a curved, prominent nose. Each time he shifted and took a breath to speak, his pince-nez spectacles, which made his squinty, pale eyes seem huge, fell from his face. Each time, as if anticipating it, he grabbed them mid-air and repositioned them with an ever-increasing, smudged thumbprint on the lens.

"Can't be far, Cap'n," said Everly, readjusting his spectacles. "Don't feel up to dealing with those sonsabitches today."

They rode between rolling hills of farmland and pastures. A soft breeze carried the scent of lilacs and pig-dung from a nearby farm. Everly winced at the smell, and Butler laughed at his aide's discomfort.

They stopped, and Butler dismounted, stretched, removed a map from his saddlebag, and began to consult it. With a shock of red hair above a freckled face, Butler was stocky and thick, boasting powerful shoulders and a short neck that seemed almost nonexistent, as emphasized by his posture as he squatted.

He knelt on one knee, brushing twigs and leaves away.

"A small company of men passed this way a short time ago," Butler said distractedly.

"Militia?"

"Continental regulars. Sloppy boot design." Butler returned the map and remounted.

"God save the king's cobblers." Everly grinned. "I'd drink a dram to the bootmakers before a bloody general any day."

"Eli…"

"Captain?"

"This is dangerous business."

"It is, sir."

"We need the men. I thought it went well."

"But Negro recruits?" Everly shook his head slowly. "Where will it end, Captain? Women fighting? They'd kick our arses and have us scrubbing the floors. God protect us."

"A man is a man, and I will take him in any color if he will fight. Let's see if we can recruit some locals at the tavern here. What say you?" Butler did not wait for Everly's reply, but spurred his horse.

****

In one corner of a small tavern, Butler sat straddling the back of a chair, his forearms draped over it. Everly stood behind him, and leaned against a wall, his arms crossed. Tobacco smoke filled the hall, creating a thick haze that hung like wet clothes on a line.

A semi-circle of skeptical local farmers eyed Butler. Their boots were muddied and their clothes soiled from the field, and each held a mug in his hand.

In the far corner, a man snored with his face on the table, long hair spread across the tabletop in tangles. The barkeep regarded the sleeping drunk once and shook his head.

"And for whom would we fight?" asked a young man in the semi-circle.

"Lieutenant-Colonel John Butler, commissioned by His Majesty to raise a regiment of rangers," replied Butler.

"We know your father, and no man here doubts either his loyalty to the king or his courage."

"Then tell me what it is you doubt, my friend."

"King George oppresses us!" exclaimed one rotund farmer, his fingers like fat pink cucumbers wrapped around a mug of ale.

"The only oppression you suffer is that of your wife's rolling pin," Butler replied with a wink to a round of laughter.

"Aye! And her damn treacherous broom," the man grumbled.

In the opposite corner, as the talk continued, the drunk stood up from the table. He watched Butler with narrowed eyes and wiped dry ale froth from his top lip. The barkeep moved quickly until he stood behind him and folded his beefy arms.

"Pay up, Angus, ye totty-headed muckworm," said the barkeep loudly.

Angus dug in his pocket and dropped a few coins into the keep's hand, then to the keep's surprise exited with a steady gait, apparently no longer under the influence of ale.

Upon leaving the tavern, he hustled to a small building several streets away. Inside, about twenty Continental soldiers, along with an officer, lounged near a stone fireplace. Angus made his way to the officer, seated comfortably in a wingback chair.

"He's in the tavern, Colonel Cummings," Angus growled, pointing through a window.

The colonel frowned. "You sure it's Walter Butler?"

"I know the man, damn you," replied Angus, hopping up and down. "And he's being a right seditious bastard, recruiting for the crown!"

A fine spray of Angus's spittle landed on Cumming's leg, who then pulled a handkerchief from inside his jacket, casually wiped it off, and stood.

"Very well," replied Cummings. "If this is some drunken fancy of yours, Angus Smith, I'll have you in the stockade before that ale in your belly turns to piss." Chuckles erupted from the soldiers. To his men he said, "I want ten deployed to the rear of the tavern. The rest of you follow me."

The colonel turned to leave, but was blocked by Angus's outstretched hand. Cummings pushed past the aggrieved man.

"I'm all out of Judas-coin today, I fear," Cummings said over his shoulder.

****

Inside the tavern, Butler and the men laughed heartily. The door burst open, and ten soldiers, muskets pointed forward, pressed into the room followed by Colonel Cummings. Butler stared down the muzzles, all with bayonets affixed. The farmers quietly melted away. Butler and Everly backed toward the rear entrance. As Butler was about to reach for the door handle, it swung open. More soldiers pushed their way into the room from the open door, their muskets also trained on the two men.

Butler smiled. He returned to his chair, swung it around, and settled firmly into it, facing the Colonel and his men. He removed his sword and placed it across his lap. He winked once at Everly, who nodded and began to inch his way toward the open door behind the soldiers.

Colonel Cummings stepped forward. "Walter Butler, you are under arrest."

"Captain Walter Butler of the King's Rangers, in flesh and in truth. On whose authority am I arrested?"

"General Benedict Arnold, and the Continental Congress."

Butler raised an eyebrow. He noticed Everly back quietly out of the room. Once he was sure Everly had successfully made his escape, a faint smile came to his lips. "And what is my offense, Colonel?"

"You're a traitor and spy to these United Colonies, sir! Your sword, please."

Butler rose slowly, took his sword and handed it, hilt first, to Cummings. He bowed, and the soldiers lowered their weapons. Cummings accepted the sword, bowing in return.

"I'll have a moment with the prisoner," he said to his men, who backed off to a respectful distance. Taking him gently by the elbow, Cummings moved to the corner of the room, then closed his eyes momentarily, took a deep breath, and opened them again.

"What in the bloody hell do you think you're doing, Walter?" he asked with a growl.

Butler grinned. "How is your wife, Joshua? Your children?"

Cummings shook his head and leaned in close, his eyes narrowing.

"You cannot come here of all places, harangue these men, and expect us to turn a blind eye."

"Ah, Joshua. Even in law school, with a pint in your fist, you were wound too tight."

The two men stared at each other as Butler reached out and patted him on the shoulder. Cummings finally broke his gaze and folded his arms in resignation, a rueful smile on his face.

"Very well. You understand I have my orders."

"We all have our orders."

****

The jail cell was little more than a five-by-five room, the floor of which was covered with straw. High up on the wall hung a window about the size of a man's head. Butler sat with his back to the bars, behind which was a larger room illuminated by several candles. The jailer was a boy still in his teen years, Butler judged.

"What's your name, Private?" He pivoted while sitting, and rested his hands on his crossed legs.

The sleepy-eyed boy seemed unsure in his brand-new private uniform, his hair tied back in a ponytail. "William, Captain," he replied.

"My name's Walter. Forget the titles."

"Yes sir. I know your name."

"You know, Billy, that I'm a dead man, right?"

"Ain't none of my business, sir." He shook his head and walked toward the cell. "Not supposed to talk to you."

Butler stood and leaned against the bars.

"You ever seen a man hang, son?"

"That I have."

"Under what circumstances?"

"My father. For treason against the king," William said, looking into Butler's eyes.

Butler winced, "Well, that was an ill-timed question if ever there was one."

William smiled and wrinkled his nose. "I hold no grudges against the King. My father was a brutal bastard and right cruel son of a bitch who deserved to hang."

Butler chuckled. He grasped the cell's bars and leaned his forehead against them.

"If I had a jug o' rum, the world would smile one last time on a wretched dead man such as me."

William hesitated. "I could be thrown into the stocks for that, Captain."

"And who will testify against you, lad, me soon to be on the wrong side o' the grass? Show a pending corpse some pity, for God's sake."

William left and returned after a bit with a jug of rum and handed it to Butler, who had to drink with his face up against the bars of the cell, since the jug was too large to fit between them. He handed it back and sat. William pulled up a stool, sat, and also drank.

"You have yourself a lass, my lad?"

"No longer, Captain. She fancies another."

"Ah. The fickle ways of the world. Cheer up, plenty more where that one came from, I promise you," said Butler. Each time he was offered the jug, he pretended to swill deeply from it, but swallowed nothing at all. William guzzled from it with gusto.

"You married, Walter?"

An image of Amanda flashed into his mind; her head

tilted back into the pillows. Her throat muscles bulged taut like iron bands, her blonde hair matted to her forehead with sweat. With only the helpless midwife and him to tend to her, she died in agony and left him with a stillborn son.

"No, the freer to sniff the blooming lilies." Butler hid his rending heart behind a generous smile. He motioned to the rum. "Drink up, my boy!"

William laughed and drank deeply. Butler sighed, turned, and placed his back against the bars of the cell. He looked up at the few visible stars that shone through the barred window and began to sing in a pure tenor voice.

On the second couplet, William sat on the floor, leaned his back against Butler's, and joined him in the song with a rusty baritone. William, Butler noticed, was clearly slurring his words.

Butler could feel William slump to the side as his singing partner's voice trailed off. He turned as William began to snore. Reaching through the bars, he carefully removed a set of keys from William's belt, which he used to open the door and quietly step over the unconscious man.

Before he left and went out into the night, he turned to his young jailer and finished the song under his breath, "For let 'em be clumsy, or let 'em be slim, young or ancient, I care not a feather; so fill a pint bumper quite up the brim, and let us e'en toast them together." He saluted, then backhanded the unconscious boy hard across the face. William didn't seem to notice. He belched and again began to snore.

"Sorry, Billy, but you'll be in enough trouble as it is. A swollen purple welt will go far to show you put up a fight." He grabbed the jug and slipped quietly out the door.

****

A gibbous moon hung in the sky, burning through the attenuated clouds that drifted overhead. Silence, but for the distant call of a loon, blanketed the dense forest of pine and maple. Trudging down a winding road, the empty jug dangled over his shoulder, his finger through its loop, Butler whistled as he walked. He knew they'd search for him in the morning, but likely wouldn't have the time or inclination to push much beyond Connecticut's border, which he was about to cross. The night's air was chilly, and all he wore were his blouse and trousers.

They'd taken his boots, the bastards.

He heard a horse's whinny far ahead and around a bend. He stepped gingerly off the path and hid behind a tree. A man on horseback, another horse tied behind, walked into the dim light of the slim moon. Butler squinted, trying to see. Then he laughed and stepped back onto the road.

"Halt, ye Limey bastard!" Butler boomed.

"Go to hell and be damned!" the man yelled back, reining his horse. The man paused, staring at Butler, then laughed as well. "If it ain't the treasonous lobcock, Captain Butler himself. I figured you'd be swinging like the tits on a threepenny upright by now. Good thing I also figured there wasn't a jail that could hold Captain Walter Butler for long, you slippery bastard."

Butler laughed as he walked up to his aide, Eli Everly, who reached in a saddle bag and tossed a pair of boots to Butler.

"Watch your tongue, Eli," said Butler with a teasing tone, yanking the boots on. He mounted the second horse and pulled in the reins.

"My tongue didn't get me court-martialed and sentenced to hang, I reckon."

"You may shove your tongue in a hairy hole. Let's be out of this broke colony."

"Colonel Butler and the Mohawk Valley?" Everly asked, raising his eyebrow, which dislodged his spectacles. He caught them with a flourish.

"Yes, let's see what Father's up to, the bristly codger. It's time to raise some hell." Butler spurred his horse, and the two men trotted off into the darkness.

Chapter 5
Blue-Axe

A nearly full waxing moon, suspended among the stars, hung over Richard and Shenandoah. They pressed forward through tall spruce and pine trees at a relaxed jog, passing the lead every once in a while. Richard's calves had begun to ache several hours ago, but he wasn't about to cede the pace to a woman, no matter how beautiful. Now in the lead, she seemed oblivious to the grueling clip, her back straight and shoulders squared even as he fought against the urge to slouch and his breath began to rattle. He needed something to take his mind off his aching muscles.

He watched her from behind, snug in her deerskin breeches. Her body swayed gracefully to the left and then to the right. Back and forth, forever, like ocean waves. Mesmerized, his breathing slowed, his mind emptied and the pain in his joints receded. He looked up at the stars above.

He tripped on something and fell hard on his face, his musket clattering on the packed dirt of the road. He turned to look—a fat porcupine stared at him with narrowed eyes as if annoyed, then waddled into the brush.

He sat up, spat out a small clod of dirt, and began to pull out the clump of quills stuck in the toe of his boot.

Shenandoah walked up to him. Her eyes twinkled in the shimmering moonlight. "If you were watching where you were going, rather than staring at the stars, you wouldn't be eating dirt."

Richard sighed. "A man can dream."

She smiled, reached her hand out, and pulled him up. He looked to the east and could make out a dim amber glow. "It's nearly morning. We need to find shelter for the day."

A quarter-mile off the road, they found a rock outcropping from a cliff that would provide shadow during the day.

Richard gathered ferns and dumped them in a small pile. "These will make a soft bed. Can you start a fire?" When she didn't answer, he looked around. Shenandoah had disappeared. He shook his head and dragged more ferns to the shelter.

He set about building a small fire, careful to keep the smoke to a minimum by using the driest possible tinder. She returned with a dead squirrel, her knife out, and quickly skinned and gutted it. They skewered it and propped it over the fire. As it cooked, sunlight began to stream through the treetops. They drank the last few dregs from a small canteen of water Shenandoah had in her backpack and ate the fire-roasted squirrel.

They licked their fingers clean of the delicious fat that the animal still hoarded from a mild winter.

He turned and moved to the bed of ferns. Lying down, he shifted to the far side below the granite overhang, and patted the open space beside him. She crossed to him, and lay down on her side with her back to him. He snuggled closer, and they embraced as a warm breeze rustled the leaves. He hugged her tightly. She reached back to run her fingers through his hair.

They hung like cocooned butterflies in a suspended place of delirium, unable to move forward and consummate their desire because every limb ached to the bone with weariness and fatigue. Both soon relented to the wave of brutal exhaustion that washed over them. She turned and kissed him gently on the cheek. Face resting against face, a deep and dreamless slumber came quickly.

Richard woke later in the afternoon. He reached for her, but she was gone. He crawled out from under the ledge, stood, and stretched. He scanned his surroundings in the daylight. It was mostly spruce, jack pine, and cedar, old growth and towering. The trees kept the undergrowth sparse, except for young ferns, moss, and scattered blueberry bushes. The air was redolent with the scent of pine and cedar.

As he looked about, he noticed a low-hanging branch on a spruce tree had been broken such that it seemed to point down a small pathway.

Shenandoah.

He followed that path down a small incline between boulders and slate outcroppings covered in moss. There was a gentle rustle of flowing water, and he came upon a clear creek that shimmered over copper-colored pebbles.

Looking downstream, she sat in the water with her naked back to him. She turned to look then glanced away. He shed his clothes and laid them carefully on the bank. He dipped his toe in the water, then yanked it back. It was icy cold. Taking a deep breath, he stepped into the ankle-deep water and sat down. He laughed at the shock to his skin and began to wash himself, using the fine sand between the pebbles to scrub away the sweat and grime. It felt like a million needles pricked his skin, and his muscles ached in protest. His heartbeat quickened, and his breathing was quick and shallow. He rinsed the last of the dirt from his head and face and felt warm hands on his back. He rose and turned.

She stood facing him and traced the indent between his pectoral muscles with a soft finger, downward, until her hand found him firm and erect. But only for a second, squeezing just enough for his legs to tremble. She removed her hand and pointed to an opening in the bushes on the far bank, took his hand, and led him across the stream.

They came into a meadow of harebell and daylily wildflowers. He wanted to plant his longing, with hers, into the meadow's breast, there to bloom forever. He caressed the skin of her back as they kissed, and pressed himself into her stomach. She held his head in her hands and twirled the tip of her wet, soft tongue in his ear, insistent, and exhaled breathy words in a language he did not understand. But he knew what she meant.

He turned her on her back, entered her, and felt the luxury of the enveloping warmth in contrast to the cool air, to the thousand tiny tongues of grass on his legs and arms, her breathing rhythmic and deep. A sudden breeze swept them from head to foot in a wave of coolness. She wrapped her legs around his backside and they moved together.

They made love until exhaustion came upon them once again, his face buried in her shoulder, neither saying a word. Thus they remained until the evening had begun to cover their naked bodies with shadows.

****

After donning their clothes, they returned to their camp as darkness settled, and they filled Shenandoah's canteen from the stream. A cloudy night kept the moon and stars at bay, so he knew their progress tonight would be slower.

Shenandoah sharpened her knife on a whetstone, eyes focused on the blade. He watched her. Her brow furrowed, her mind apparently a thousand miles away. Each snick of the blade along the stone followed a breath, and each breath followed a slight tip of her head to the side, so that her curls bobbed. The simple rhythm of it seemed to correspond to his heartbeat, to the ancient rhythm of…lovemaking. He was getting aroused.

"Was that your…first time?" he asked. He scratched his temple and let his arms drop to his side. He regretted asking.

She looked up and stared at him. Her couldn't read her face, which was hidden in shadow. "Was it yours? If it was, you did ok, Captain Dick." She sheathed her knife, picked up her bag, and headed back toward the trail.

Warmth crept up his neck. He closed his eyes and shook his head. *She's right. I am a fool.* He grabbed the muskets and ran to catch up with her.

They followed a trail and came upon several small villages that were nothing more than an inn and a few huts, carefully skirted them, and then returned to the road once again. His body began to adjust to the strain until he no longer felt pains or aches as they ran, just a brilliant joy, his arms swinging freely and legs catching his weight with ease each step forward that he took. As the sun rose, they kept moving farther than the previous night, until the morning came and the air began to warm.

The trail they were on curved and ran parallel to a wide and deep river. Richard knew they would have to cross it eventually to continue north, and began to look for a bridge or fordable narrowing. He eyed the waters nervously as they jogged. The childhood memory of drowning, of water forcing its way into his lungs, flashed briefly, accompanied as always by the guttural growl of a lion. He shook his head to try and throw the images out like one would throw the contents of a bedpan. His eyes focused on the tip of his nose. It remained fixed as the world flew past him and changed in ways he couldn't always understand.

While he was fixated on a drop of sweat hanging from the tip of his nose, Shenandoah tapped him on the shoulder. They stopped and she pointed to a bridge ahead. He nodded, and they approached it slowly, carefully checking their surroundings.

As they got closer, he could see the bridge was built with wet pine, braced in a pattern that made no sense. It was narrow, and not particularly sturdy or well-built. A Black man appeared from under it. His arms were huge, wrapped in heavy muscle, and his legs shot down to the ground as if they grew from roots. On his back was strapped a heavy blue axe.

He blocked the entrance to the bridge, folded his arms, and regarded them with narrowed eyes. Richard glanced at Shenandoah. She shrugged. Richard nodded; they would have to deal with the giant. He stepped forward.

"Hello, friend," Richard said calmly.

The giant didn't move or flinch.

"We need to cross that bridge." More silence. "My name's Richard. You can call me Captain Dick. What's your name?"

"They call me Blue Axe." Blue unfolded his arms and pointed at the bridge. "You wanna cross, you pay my toll."

"I see. That your bridge, is it?"

"Built it with my own hands."

"It's a helluva bridge."

"Damn right," Blue said, nodding.

"What's the toll?" asked Richard, moving closer.

Blue narrowed his eyes and pondered.

"What you got?"

"Ain't got nothing."

"You runaways. You stole something when you run; we always do."

"Told you, we got nuthin'."

Blue scratched his chin and pointed at the muskets.

"You got them Brown Besse's."

"Nope. Can't have 'em."

Blue shrugged. "You can swim, you can pay my toll, or you can try to smash through me. Ain't no other choices."

Richard looked at Shenandoah, his eyebrow raised.

"Swim?" she asked.

"Can't swim," he replied.

Her eyes widened, surprised. He handed her the muskets and his backpack. He glanced around and noticed a stripped pine branch left over from the earlier bridge construction. It was three inches thick and about six feet long. He hefted it and looked down its length.

This'll do just fine.

"Was hoping you'd choose that," Blue said, watching Richard approach him.

Richard swung the stick in broad circles, limbering up. He'd fought with a similar staff years ago when he first came to this country, taught by a field slave from Bini. Blue folded his arms once again, unimpressed. Richard stopped about ten feet in front of him.

44

"Let me ask you a question," said Richard.

"Yeah?"

"What you gonna do when the White man shows up, laughs at your toll, shoots you dead, and then takes your bridge?"

Blue furrowed his brow, confused. As he glanced back to look at the bridge, Richard struck. The branch hit Blue's shoulder with a loud *crack* and split in half. He dropped the useless half as Blue staggered to the left, then he dove and tackled Blue at the knees.

The two struggled up against the flimsy railing of the bridge until Blue picked Richard up by the waist as though he weighed no more than a feather, and held him over the railing. Richard beat his fists against Blue's back. It was like beating on a sack of bricks—he was damaging his own hands. Blue grunted once, and then tossed him casually in the river.

Richard fell and splashed into the middle of the water. He sunk down deep, scraping his forehead against the river bottom. He surfaced, coughing and sputtering, his arms flailing. Blue looked over the edge, curious, and watched the ungainly spectacle.

"Damn," he said, then turned and yelled to Shenandoah. "He can't swim!"

Shenandoah was already headed to the riverbank. She dove in head-first, swam to Richard, grabbed him by the scruff of his collar from behind as his arms swung about like a windmill, and dragged him back to the shore. Coughing, Richard went limp as if in a daze. Shenandoah struggled to pull him up, his weight more than she could manage. She looked up. Blue towered above them, his arm extended. She reached up. He grabbed it, took Richard by the shoulder with his other hand,

and easily pulled both of them up and onto the bank like drowned cats.

****

The three sat beneath the shade of an apple tree on the far bank of the river in the early afternoon. Blue sharpened his axe with a long whetstone.

"So, you a captain?" Blue asked.

Richard looked up from the map he had been studying. Shenandoah sat beside him, whittling a stick with her knife.

"No. My last owner was."

"He dead?"

"No." Richard pointed to the axe in Blue's lap. "I guess you know how to use that."

"You guess right."

"Why's the handle blue?"

"Why's the sky blue?"

Richard considered and frowned. Shenandoah laughed under her breath. Blue nodded to Shenandoah.

"She don't speak much, do she?"

"Nope," answered Richard.

"What's her name?"

"Shenandoah," she said without looking up from her knife.

"Pleased to meet ya, ma'am. Where you folks headed?"

"New York frontier," replied Richard, looking back down at his map.

Blue grunted, then whistled under his breath. "Butler's Rangers," he said.

Richard nodded, his eyes widening. He was impressed

that Blue knew about Butler and the Rangers.

"Need some company?"

"What about your bridge?" asked Richard.

"That ain't my bridge. I just tell people it's mine so I can take their money. Whoever built that bridge don't know shit about bridges."

"I figured. Your master dead?"

"Yup."

"I figured."

"I just wanna be a free man." Blue held his huge hand out, palm up. "War's started. We choose the right side, we win the prize. Why you wanna fight?"

Richard stared for a moment at the shavings that fell from the stick as Shenandoah's knife sliced it rhythmically down to nothing.

"I still remember my mother being violated, and cut into pieces by machetes in front of me," Richard began, staring into the distance. "Her blood was on my face and chest." He ran his fingers over his face. "It was warm and it smelled like iron. They dragged me, a bloody, screaming, biting little boy to the slave ship. I ain't done biting yet."

Richard glanced at Shenandoah, then looked Blue dead in the eyes. He put his hand out in Blue's. Shenandoah put her hand on top of both men's.

"Free or dead," said Richard.

"Free or dead," repeated Shenandoah and Blue.

Richard withdrew his hand, picked up one of the muskets, and handed it to Blue.

"Ever fire one?"

"Nope. But I learn quick."

"I guess you do. White men catch us, they're gonna do a whole lot worse than just kill us."

"Ain't nuthin' worse than bein' a slave your whole life."

Richard nodded. After replacing his axe on his back, Blue hefted the musket admiringly, running his rugged palm over the stock and barrel.

"White folk see slaves in the middle of the road with weapons in their hand, they likely to pee on themselves," said Blue distractedly.

Shenandoah and Richard laughed as the three stood beneath the tree. Richard picked up the remaining musket, Shenandoah sheathed her knife, and they made their way into dense woods to hide for the day.

Chapter 6
Zion

Three Black men with their hands tied behind them were roped by the neck and tethered together. They shuffled wearily down the road. A White man on horseback with the neck-rope tied to his saddle's pommel led the way. A second White man followed behind with a musket; both wore Continental Army Regular uniforms.

Richard, Shenandoah, and Blue squatted, hidden behind a clump of trees about fifty yards distant near the crest of a hill and watched the procession. Richard pointed to the back of the line, then to the man on horseback. Blue and Shenandoah moved off, low to the ground, in different directions.

Richard returned his attention to the procession in the distance. The first hostage was a muscular man in dirty, torn rags. His face was battered, one eye blackened and swollen shut, with numerous cuts and scrapes around his neck and shoulders. He had put up a good fight when they captured that one.

The second man was older, perhaps in his fifties. He wore Native Ojibwe clothing that consisted of a simple breechclout and moccasins, light brown tunic with beads and feathers. He limped with each step, as if his left leg was slightly shorter than his right.

The third prisoner was thin and young, dressed as an English gentleman: fine waistcoat, embroidered linen shirt, high-quality breeches, and knee-high boots. They were soiled now and well-worn but had once been fit for a nobleman. A well-groomed goatee gave him a haughty appearance, even in such extremity.

"Don't know about you chaps, but I could certainly use a pint of grog about now, wot," called the third prisoner. They trudged forward in silence. "Excuse me," he called more loudly to the man on horseback. "I told you, there's been a mistake here. I'm a freeman. I seem to have lost my papers, true, but I really must insist that you let me go."

The White man in the back ran up and smacked him hard on the hip with the butt of his weapon. "Keep movin' and shut yer mouth," he said, giving the muscular man a smack as well, and then the limping man for good measure. Satisfied with his brief beatings, he returned to take up the rear.

The muscular man turned his head to the gentleman behind him. "The hell is wrong with you?"

"Walk and be silent—for now," said the limping man, who appeared to be staring directly at Richard. Richard moved down from the hill, crouching low as he made his way.

The man on horseback yanked on the rope, causing all three to stumble. They recovered and settled into a dull rhythm, eyes cast down.

Richard stepped out from behind a clump of bushes, his musket in the crook of his arm. The procession halted as the trailing White man ran to the front. The man on horseback dismounted.

"What the hell?" The man with the musket spat.

"Lord Almighty, nigger with a musket," said the second, eyes wide.

Richard strode forward confidently and stopped about thirty feet in front of them. "Gentlemen, put the musket on the ground, please."

After a pause wherein nobody moved, the man began to furiously load the musket, powder-horn shaking.

"Don't do that," Richard said, shaking his head and waving his arm.

Off to the side, Blue stepped out from behind a huge oak tree, the musket at his shoulder pointed forward. The weapon suddenly went off with a boom, the musket ball going wild and high, causing everyone, including Richard, to duck. The musket flew out of Blue's hands and landed on the ground about ten feet to the side of him.

"Well, goddamn it. Didn't mean to do that," said Blue.

Richard yanked his musket to his shoulder and pointed it at the soldier still frantically loading his weapon. "That was a warning," he said, cocking the hammer. "Next one goes in your gut."

The man slowly set the gun on the ground and stood, his hands up. The second man raised his hands.

Shenandoah emerged from bushes on the opposite side of the road, removed her knife, and cut the ropes binding the hostages. Blue came up and grabbed the musket that the White man had set on the ground as Richard approached the group.

As Shenandoah cut the rope from the gentleman's hands, he bowed slightly.

"Much appreciated, madam," he said.

Richard moved to the horse, grabbed a large sack tied to the pommel, and looked inside. "Bread and a side of salted beef." He handed the sack to the limping man, then grabbed a corked crock also tied to the saddle. He popped the cork, sniffed, and smiled. Rum.

The gentleman grinned. "I'd be more than willing to

carry that, sir."

Richard recorked it and handed it to him.

"Get up," Richard said to the two soldiers, motioning toward the horse. The men clambered onto the steed.

"You just gonna let 'em go? And take the horse with them?" the muscular man asked, eyes wide.

"We travel light, don't need any horses to worry about," said Richard. The muscular man folded his arms.

"Who the hell are you?" one of the White men asked Richard.

"The name's Captain Dick."

"We're from the Third Connecticut Provincial Regiment under Colonel Putnam. These men are recruits for the Continental Army. This is treason, and you'll all hang, boy."

"Rebelling against your king is treason. We're only rebelling against you. Ride on before I change my mind."

"You heard him. Now git!" yelled Blue. He slapped the horse's rear.

The horse jumped forward and trotted down the road. Shenandoah picked up a small stone and threw it. It hit one of the men a glancing blow on the back of the head. He yelped.

The muscular man took his first close look at Shenandoah. Richard saw their eyes meet, and she quickly turned away, drawing a smirk from the man.

The group formed a loose circle.

"Many thanks, sir! A true Squire Robin of the Hood. Where are you headed?" the gentleman asked Richard.

"The northern frontier."

"Well, I have no pressing engagements. Perhaps you'll allow me to accompany you. I can cook, and I never miss a chance to tell a good story."

"Son of a bitch never shuts up," grumbled the muscular man.

The man in moccasins stepped forward.

"I live with a tribe in the Mohawk Valley. They can take us in, at least for a while. The Rangers move through regularly, and we have a truce with Colonel Butler," he said.

"Butler? Butler's Rangers?" asked the muscular man. "Now why do you think Colonel Butler is gonna let a bunch of raggedy-arsed fools fight with him?"

"I beg your pardon. 'Raggedy-arsed?'" interjected the gentleman.

"That's the plan. But suit yourself. War is coming, and if we choose wisely, we'll be free men with land of our own," replied Richard.

The muscular man offered his hand to Richard. "Guess there's no better place to go. Name's Hallelujah, but call me Lou." Richard shook his hand.

"Captain Dick. This is Shenandoah."

"She your woman?" asked Lou.

"You talk to me when you have a question," said Shenandoah.

"Yes, ma'am. You his woman?" asked Lou.

"Ain't nobody's woman but my own." Shenandoah turned and walked away.

"Always was, always will be," Lou muttered under his breath.

Richard stared at him, confused by Lou's apparent familiarity with Shenandoah.

"I'm Ben Franklin," said the gentleman, interrupting

the awkward silence.

Richard blinked and frowned. He had heard of Franklin, and this Black man was definitely not him.

"It was not my idea, I can assure you. My former owner was a friend and admirer of Mr. Franklin and had a dry sense of humor."

"Blue," said Blue.

"My village is Iroquois and four days that direction," said the limping man, pointing. "Not much food between here and there. Local militia is active now and will be mad as swatted hornets."

Richard nodded and moved in the direction indicated. The rest of the group followed.

"What's your name, friend?" Richard asked as they walked.

"Steps-in-Holes," the limping man said, sighing.

Richard laughed. "Course it is."

****

Two men in gentlemen's attire entered a run-down and dimly-lit tavern. They looked around in dismay, and sighed simultaneously. The appointments were mostly ramshackle, dirty, with peanut shells and smeared vomit on the floor. A few semi-conscious patrons lay face down on the tables in front of them.

Titus Hosmer, a lawyer from Middletown, Connecticut and a delegate to the Continental Congress, was a diminutive man with a long horse-face and petite, fluttering hands. The second man was John Alsop, a wealthy merchant and politician from New York, who also happened to be a delegate to the

Congress. He was portly and robust, with a ruddy glow to his features.

Alsop pointed to a small table in the corner, and the two sat after Titus had meticulously dusted his chair's seat with a handkerchief. A fat barkeeper with a stained leather apron approached, plonked two mugs on the table, and wandered away without saying a word. Using his handkerchief, Titus pushed the mug to the side with two fingers as if it were hot to the touch.

Alsop laughed, grabbed his mug, and took a giant swig. "Really, Titus," he said, wiping his mouth with his sleeve, "this is certainly colorful."

"If you catch the pox, don't blame me," replied Titus, shaking his head.

"Hmmm. Now see here, I haven't all night to waste. Your man will be here?"

"Yes, he should be here any moment."

Alsop took another swig. "Excellent. Skullduggery is such fun!"

The tavern door opened, and Captain Lucius Prescott entered, wearing civilian attire. His face was pasty and splotched, his unwashed hair matted and tangled. He noticed the two men in the corner who stood as he approached.

"John, this is Captain Prescott. Captain, may I introduce the Honorable John Alsop of New York," said Titus.

"An honor, sir," said Prescott as the two men shook hands. He then grabbed a nearby chair and sat next to the other two men.

"I've heard a great deal about the success of your business," began Prescott, "And I—"

"Captain, I haven't the time. Titus tells me you have a

proposition," said Alsop. He finished off his mug and plunked it on the table.

"Certainly. I propose to locate and infiltrate Colonel Butler's Rangers. It should be easy to assassinate Colonel Butler and his vexing son, Captain Butler. That would remove a troublesome thorn from your New York skin. Quick enough?"

The barkeep returned and set a full mug in front of Alsop and Prescott. Titus peered over the lip of Prescott's mug, then into his own.

He sighed.

"Indeed," Alsop said. "But only in the telling. I suppose you have a plan."

"He does. But he needs the funds promptly," said Titus.

"Don't we all. Go on," said Alsop impatiently.

Prescott leaned in close and glanced at each man. His eyes narrowed.

"I intend to gather a group of five or six hand-picked men, masquerade as Loyalists, seek out the Rangers and offer our services."

Alsop snorted ale onto the table. It bubbled and frothed. Titus blanched and pushed back from the table when the regurgitated ale began to drip on his leg.

"Butler will find you out in a heartbeat," boomed Alsop. "They are watching closely for traitors. What, you think he's a simpleton? You think I'm a simpleton?"

"John, please. I'll help him in this matter, you have my word," said Titus, his hands raised.

"In exchange for my vote in Congress and my money."

"Votes for favors. Thus it was and thus it always will be." Titus picked up his mug with his handkerchief and tentatively took a sip.

"I can do this," said Prescott, leaning back.

"Tell me something, Captain."

"Yes?"

"Would this idea of yours have anything to do with your recent runaway? Poorpoint or some such?"

"Pierpoint. And absolutely not."

"Good. Because if it does, if there are motives here that work contrary to my best interests and to the interests of Congress, I'll ruin you. Do you understand, sir?"

"I do indeed. I can assure you that—"

"Excellent. By all means, rid us of those glory-seeking, Negro-loving, king's toadies, the Butlers." Alsop raised his mug, and the three toasted.

"Here, here!" cheered Prescott.

"Then glory and prosperity to these United Colonies," said Titus. "And may the tyrant George tumble down the steps of the Tower and break his bloody neck." All three finished their mugs and slammed them on the table.

Titus stared balefully into the bottom of his mug. "Good Lord, I believe there's a rat-tail in mine."

****

Richard and his crew pushed northward. They had begun to move during the day, which, although increasing the likelihood of meeting others on the roads, quickened their progress. Or so Richard hoped.

"You need to teach us to load and shoot these things. We can't be hiding all the time," Lou said to Richard, as he eyed down the sight of a musket.

"I will, but right now we need food."

"Two more days until we reach my settlement," interjected Steps. "Not far from here is a Christian mission run by a minister and his wife. They should have food to share."

"It's safe?" asked Richard.

Steps shrugged. "As safe as any Christian can be, I suppose. You can never know for sure with them which way their bible points: one day it's mercy, the next day it's killing."

"Your settlement?," asked Blue. "My head spinning. Iroquois, Mohawk, Oneida. Who you belong to and which side are they on?"

"Iroquois is the six-nations. Mohawk is my people. They stand with the king. Oneida are also Iroquois, but they're another band of people, and they fight for the Americans."

"Alright," Richard said. "Which way?"

Steps pointed and the merry band trudged off. Richard led now.

They walked for the better part of an hour under a blistering sun. The mission was a small wooden building—part home and part chapel—with a cross that rose from its roof. About fifty yards away sat a large barn with gray, weathered wooden sides and a chained and padlocked double-door in the front.

The crew stood on a rocky hill overlooking the property. As they made their way down the slope, Shenandoah put her hand over her mouth and nose and gasped. Seeing Shenandoah's reaction, they all stopped and sniffed the air.

"What the hell is *that*?" asked Lou, coughing. "Smells like a whore's—"

"That be death," said Steps.

"Let's go," said Richard. He led the way down the hill. He watched warily as they descended. The smell made the hairs on the back of his arms stand on end.

They stood in the main yard of the mission and looked around. A broken-down, abandoned wagon, some children's toys in a small pile, and another pile of half-burned adult clothing lay about the ground. Near the house was a newly turned grave, a crude cross planted at the head and draped with a ring of faded flowers.

"Hello? Anybody here?" Richard yelled. A broken and spinning windmill clicked and dinged.

"It's coming from there," Ben said, pointing to the barn. He wrinkled his nose and covered his face with the crook of his arm.

Richard walked toward it, the others trailing behind. He put his hand on the padlocked chain across the door. He caught Blue's eyes, nodded, and stepped back. Blue unlimbered his axe, swung it and smashed the rusty lock. Sparks flew. The lock tumbled to the ground, and the chain slipped through the brass handles.

Richard took a deep breath, held it, pulled the door open and stepped into the dark interior. The others followed him, one by one.

Rays of sunlight streamed through broken roof slats to illuminate a scene from hell. The dead bodies of Black men, women, and children lay in various poses of agony about the floor on rotting and bloody piles of straw or small wooden crates and cots. Their pockmarked skin oozed with pustules and open wounds. The palpable stench pressed into Richard's nose and mouth. He gagged as it slithered down his esophagus, and twisted his gut with nausea. He held his breath, not wanting to take one more inhalation until he could calm his churning stomach.

"Smallpox," Richard said under his breath, finally releasing his lungful of air.

Steps lunged forward and grabbed Ben's hand as he reached toward a dead woman on a cot. Her hair was matted, skin swollen, but her eyes stared ahead from a peaceful face.

"Don't touch anything! Everybody out. Now!" growled Steps.

They stumbled out of the barn, gagging and coughing. Ben leaned over and retched.

"Oh my God..." gurgled Ben.

Shenandoah sat on the ground, holding her legs, and rocked. Fat tears pooled in the corner of her eyes, and threatened to tumble down her cheeks. She wiped them away with the sleeve of her shirt.

Wiping the vomit from his mouth, Ben knelt beside her and held her by the shoulders.

"Richard..." Shenandoah said, her voice shaking.

But Richard was gone when she turned to look. Musket in hand and his back to them, he marched toward the church. She ran after him, and the others followed behind. Blue stumbled and used his axe, which he still hadn't put away, to right himself. Steps helped Ben, who leaned on his shoulder—a limping man steadying a man with two good, but rubbery, legs.

Richard kicked the door. He flung a cart of dirty linens to the side, then stopped and looked around as the rest pushed in behind him.

On his right were a few primitive wooden pews and a

whitewashed altar covered in dust. On the left was a modest living area, including a table covered with soiled pottery and rags. The room was silent except for the rhythmic creak of the chair as it rocked slowly back and forth.

Near a large window, a man sat in a rocking chair, his back to them.

As Richard approached him, he could see he wore a minister's frock, dirty and stained. His hair was white, long and tangled in knots. Coming around to the front, Richard saw the minister's eyes were closed. He sang something unintelligible under his breath. He opened his eyes and then his mouth as if in a silent scream, his tongue swollen.

The minister eyed Richard, the fingers of his hands fluttering like an injured bird in his lap.

"Go away," the minister said in a thick voice.

They stood in a tight circle around him.

Richard clenched his fists. "What happened here?"

"You aren't sick. I have nothing to give you." He closed his eyes and began to rock and sing again.

Richard jammed his foot against the rocker, stopping the motion, and raised his musket to point at the man's chest. "Who are you?" Richard asked, his voice rising. "Who are *they*?" He pointed toward the barn.

The minister looked in the direction Richard indicated, then sighed.

"Show respect. You are in the Lord's house, sir."

Richard lowered his musket. "Don't care about the Lord right now. What happened here?"

The minister looked around at the others, as if only now realizing there were more people in the room. A fit of coughing, hoarse and ragged, came over him. After a moment, he composed himself.

"They came from the British camps, corpses walking and oozing blood. They were searching, searching for Zion. They are the lost tribe of Israel!"

"Zion?"

"Home."

"What British camps are you talking about?"

"The British military garrisons in New York," the minister said, sitting up. A bit of color came to his cheeks. "Lord Dunmore's bloody proclamation. Freedom from their miserable bondage. So they came by the thousands. Except the British can barely feed, house and clothe themselves, let alone a horde of freed slaves. So there they rot in squalor until visited by the pox like a plague. And then they come here, desperate for salvation, for comfort. My wife and I have so little, but we did what we could."

"Why here? And where is your wife?" asked Steps.

The minister's eyes unfocused as he stared past them all and through the window at the newly dug grave.

"We stand at a crossroad. This is the edge of the Mohawk Valley, the edge of civilization. Beyond is Niagara and the western wilderness that goes on and on—perhaps forever." He leaned forward and seized the end of Richard's musket, shoving it deep into his own chest, his eyes open now and gleaming.

"You must burn it, burn it all! Cleanse everything in God's eyes! Promise you'll bury me beside my wife, then burn *everything* to the eternal earth. Now kill me, let me die!"

Richard yanked the barrel from his hands and stepped

back along with the others.

"Why should we help you?" asked Lou with a sneer. "These are your demons, the White man's demons, not ours."

"Please, I beg you. For the love of Christ Almighty, help me!"

They stood in silence. Lou spat on the floor and folded his arms.

With no hesitation, before anyone could move or object, Shenandoah stepped forward from behind the minister and slipped the tip of her knife up through the base of his skull and spine, deep into his brain.

She placed her other palm over the minister's forehead and eyes, leaned in, and whispered, "Shhhh…"

His body convulsed for the last time, and his breathing stopped.

She withdrew her knife, wiped the blood with a rag from the top of a nearby table and, in turn, stared each one of the shocked men in the eye.

"He tried to help them," she said quietly, then sheathed her knife, turned and moved as if she were going to leave the room.

Lou lunged forward, grabbed her arm from behind, and spun her around.

"What the hell do you think you're doing?" he growled in her face.

In one smooth, lightning fast movement, she pulled the knife from its sheath. Lou glanced down to see her knife between them, its tip pressing against his windpipe.

Richard didn't know if he should intervene on Shenandoah's behalf, or Lou's.

"Let me go or die," she said, her voice even and controlled.

"You tellin' me what to do, woman?"

"I'm tellin' you what *not* to do. You got that, Hallelujah?"

Richard set his musket down, grabbed Lou by the shoulders, and dragged him away from Shenandoah. Lou spun around and swung a fist at him, but it went wide, connecting with nothing but air. Richard slammed him against the wall, his forearm pressed hard against his throat. They stood so close, face to face, that Richard could smell Lou's breath, and the rum he had obviously been drinking.

"Don't ever touch her again," said Richard.

Lou calmed his breathing and unclenched his fists.

"So, who's the boss 'round here?" He sneered. "She the boss, or is you the boss, Captain? 'Cause it sure looks to me like she the boss."

Richard released his grip and stepped back.

Lou looked to the others in the group. "What you think? Think it's time for a new boss?"

Blue sauntered over to stand behind Richard and Shenandoah, his arms folded. Ben and Steps followed suit and the five stared back at Lou. Apparently assessing his quick defeat, he shrugged and smiled.

"What now, Cap'n Dick?"

****

Near sundown, Lou and Blue dug a second grave beside the first. Their noses and mouths were covered with portions of a torn sheet. Beside them lay the minister's body, wrapped in a canvas. Careful to use the canvas and not to touch the body, they laid him in the grave and began to fill it. Steps, Ben, and Richard came up to help them with their work, also masked.

As they worked, Shenandoah walked to the barn and slipped inside. She looked around, eyes wide. It was silent, and nothing stirred. The sound of death.

She walked to the corpse of a woman on a cot in the corner and stared down at her. Her face was disfigured by pox, yet still, Shenandoah could tell that she had been beautiful in life: high forehead and cheekbones, full lips, and a strong chin.

She removed a carved wooden talisman on a leather loop from around her neck and placed it gently on the dead woman's chest. She reached her hand out to brush a strand of hair away from the woman's ravaged face, then caught herself and pulled back. She took one last look around and turned to leave. Almost out the door, she heard a rustling from the direction of the dead woman. She turned, expecting the woman to rise up like Lazarus from the story the Christians had told her about, but, of course, nothing happened. She shook her head, still unused to the stench, slipped out the door and closed it behind her.

A fire burned in front of the barn as the sun set. They stood around it in a circle and watched the flames. Richard leaned down, took the cool end of a flaming birch from the fire, and walked to the barn—the entire base of which was circled with piles of loose hay. The other five each took up a flaming stick and followed him. They lit the hay until the entire circumference of the building was on fire, then gathered in the front to watch the conflagration.

Three quarters of the barn were now fully consumed as

the fire raged. Shenandoah stood transfixed, her face illuminated by the orange glow and her skin absorbing the radiated heat. The others stood far back, talking amongst themselves. She glanced behind her to look at them, the heat now nearly unbearable, then turned back one last time to look at the barn.

The small doors to the loft above the big main door swung open.

Outlined by the flames and smoke behind, a little girl stood clutching a doll, wearing the talisman that Shenandoah had left, and stared back at her.

Shenandoah screamed. Fighting against the brutal heat, she moved closer, opening her arms.

"Jump! Jump!"

But the little girl was gone.

Richard grabbed her by the shoulders and pulled her back. Her eyes watered, her skin nearly on fire.

"Help her! Help her!" she yelled.

Richard picked up a shovel, and Blue grabbed his axe. They ran to the gate of the barn as the others watched helplessly. Richard tried to pry open the door with the shovel and Blue swung his axe at its center. It blew open with a great billow of cinders and threw both men back. They stumbled and coughed, with pieces of their clothing on fire and their hair smoking. Blue dropped his axe and used his huge hands to help beat out the flames that had ignited Richard's pant legs.

Steps and Ben grabbed Shenandoah, holding her back as she twisted and squirmed, trying to rush to the flames.

The crew stood frozen, far back from the barn, as the flames completely engulfed it. Timbers fell one by one until the barn roof collapsed with a roar, as a huge ball of embers and cinders exploded upward into the night sky. Shenandoah turned away and held her arms around herself, shaking. Ash fell around them like snow.

She collapsed on the ground. Soft white flakes settled on her face and shoulders.

****

The first tendrils of morning light skimmed the trees surrounding the mission. Shenandoah hadn't moved from her sitting position. Her face, hair, and shoulders were nearly white from fallen ash. Richard approached her with a cloth, dropped to one knee beside her, and gently wiped ash from her hair and face. She reached out and clutched his arm. He looked up to stare at the smoking ruin, which was now a pile of twisted, charred timbers, coals, ash, and the last soft swirls of smoke. He stood and offered her his hand. She ignored it and pulled herself to her feet as the others gathered around. He put his arm around her.

"We need to move. People are gonna come and investigate the smoke from the fire," he said. Looking at the rubble, he added, "Wasn't anything we could do…"

She shoved him away from her.

"There never is," she shouted at all of them, her face twisted in rage. "Ain't nothin' nobody can ever do, is there? For her or for us. We just get used up and die, nothin' to do about it except hang our heads. What are you doin' about it? Or you? Any of us? None of us do nothin'. That old White man in the ground and his wife did somethin'," she said, pointing.

They looked at each other in silence and scuffed their feet like children.

"That's right," she continued. "Look at yourselves. Buncha do-nothin' niggahs ain't got no home, ain't got no family, just got your do-nothin' songs 'bout the shackles you drag around with you."

"What you want us to do?" Richard mumbled.

"Put a sword in your hand and some goddamn trouble in your heart." She pointed to the smoldering remains of the barn. "Do somethin' like fire would do."

More silence as the men stood motionless and stared at her. She sighed and picked up her things. As she did, the sun, at last, burst over the top of the trees, and slant rays of light shone like a beacon toward the northwest.

Silently, they gathered their belongings, turned away from the mission, and once again began their trek to the Mohawk Valley, now near. Overhead, Richard watched a bald eagle circle twice, then soar across the treetops.

Chapter 7
The Elixir of Life

They made their way through dense forests and open meadows dotted with purple asters. They circled around the skirts of craggy mountains and walked beside crystal-clear rivers and streams. Hungry now, they shot at deer, pheasants, squirrels and even an elk, but they always missed. At last they stopped to make camp at a clearing overlooking an emerald lake.

As night came, Shenandoah made her way down a narrow path to the lake with several wineskins. She knelt and began to fill them. Behind her, in the distance, flickered a small campfire, which gave the water an eerie yellow glow. They had decided to light it, despite the risk, because of the chill in the air.

A branch cracked, and she turned quickly, knife out.

"Whoa, whoa," said Lou, his arms held up defensively.

She sheathed her knife and returned to her task. He looked along the shore, then bent and gathered up a handful of stones. He leaned against a dogwood tree, the branches of which hung out over the shoreline, and tossed the pebbles leisurely out into the water.

"Need some help?" he asked.

She didn't reply, and he scattered a few more stones.

"You haven't told him, have you?"

"Nothing to tell," she said without looking at him.

"Well, if it were me, I'd want to know..."

Now she stood suddenly, her face in his.

"It ain't you, is it? It never was you. Never will be you."

He smiled and stepped back as he tossed a few more

stones.

"When you run, master beat me near to death. Never said a word, never gave you up."

She hesitated, staring at him, then looked up the long path to the flickering fire. "And I'm s'posed to be grateful..." She looked back at him. "Well, I am grateful. Thank you. But that was two years ago and a long ways away. What happened between us happened to two different people in a different place."

He reached out and placed a hand on her shoulder. "Ain't so different now. We're loose, but we ain't free yet."

She brushed his hand from her shoulder and gathered her full skins.

"You leave it, Hallelujah. You leave it right here." She turned away and walked up the path to the camp.

He watched her backside as his tight fist ground the stones together. He turned to the lake, reached his arm back, and flung the remaining pebbles with all his strength. They scattered and fell into the water.

Shenandoah came to the campfire and hung her skins from a nearby branch. The men lounged around the flame in a circle. Richard watched her settle beside him, remove her knife and a small whetstone, and begin to sharpen the blade with a furious *knick, knick, knick*. He looked up and saw Lou come out of the darkness also from the direction of the lake, a scowl on his face. Lou sat beside a small stump, his head hung low.

Ben pulled his jug of spirits from a sack, popped the cork, drank deeply, and passed it to Blue, who likewise passed it around the circle. When it came to Lou, he drank, passed it to Steps, and glared at Richard.

"Sure be nice if we had us some food, Captain Dick, sir," Lou said and spat into the fire.

"We gonna get some tomorrow, right?" asked Blue. "I'm hungry, too."

"Steps says one more day's walk to his village. We'll eat," Richard said, taking his turn at the jug.

He passed it to Shenandoah, who wouldn't drink, and she passed it back to Ben.

"Uh huh. Says you," muttered Lou.

"We may have no food, sir," said Ben, holding up the jug. "But we have the very elixir of life!"

"Licks her?" asked Blue, puzzled.

"Drink! But beware, gentlemen, and lady!" Ben struck an actor's pose and began to recite. "Drink, sirs, is a great provoker of three things." He paused, looking around at the upturned curious faces, but no one took the bait. He sighed. "Very well. What three things, you ask? Why, sirs, nose-painting, sleep, and urine."

"Nose-painting?" asked Steps.

"Drinking makes White men's noses turn red," said Richard dryly.

Blue squeezed his eyes shut and laughed.

"Lechery, sirs, it provokes and unprovokes. It provokes the desire, but it takes away the performance. Therefore, much drink may be said to be an equivocator with lechery. It makes him, and it mars him. It sets him on, and it takes him off. It persuades him, and disheartens him, makes him stand to and not stand to. In conclusion, equivocates him in a sleep, and, giving him the lie, leaves him," Ben finished with a flourish and a bow.

He waited for applause. Silence.

"The hell was that?" asked Blue, his fat nose scrunched up.

"That hell, sir, was Shakespeare. A noted poet and playwright, though perhaps not noted by you," answered Ben, sitting down, his shoulders drooping. He pulled out a thick book from his sack and held it up. "He wrote these plays."

"Okay, okay," said Blue. "But what did he mean?"

Ben took another swig to empty the jug. He stared at the fire, defeated.

Richard chuckled. "I think it means liquor gives you the desire to strum a lady but takes away the ability," said Richard. "Gets you hard and then makes you soft."

"Ain't never had that problem," said Blue, shaking his head. "Spear-Shaker, you said?"

"Oh, dear Lord…" moaned Ben.

"Where'd you learn this stuff?" asked Blue, genuinely curious.

"I read books! I spent one entire year studying at the University of Oxford in England. Well, I wasn't actually allowed to be a student, but I did sneak into a closet in the back of classes."

"How'd an educated niggah end up here?" asked Blue, amazed.

"That's a long story. My master sold me to an American."

"Why'd he do that? You ain't worth your price, with readin' and all that fancy stuff? Rather than haulin' a tobacco bale or cleanin' out a shit-hole?" asked Lou.

"Well, to be honest… There was a teensy bit of marital indiscretion that I was involved in."

"You laid your master's wife?" asked Lou, wide-eyed.

The circle stared at Ben.

"God damn!" said Blue, grinning.

"Not exactly…"

"Not exactly?" asked Richard. "You aimed and missed?"

"Actually, I was owned by the lady of the house. She's the one who was upset with my dalliance with her husband and sold me. If you catch my meaning."

"Oh," said Richard.

"I can assure you, it wasn't my idea. I fancy the ladies. But…it was my chance to learn to read, to go to school…"

"Man's gotta do what a man's gotta do," said Blue, nodding.

"Just so," agreed Ben.

They stared at the fire for a minute.

"I'm going to visit Paris and Athens and Rome," said Ben, his eyes transfixed by the flickering flame. "I'm going to read every bloody book in the godforsaken world. Then I'm going to write my own books. Now that is what freedom means to me, gentlemen."

Blue turned the jug, now in his possession, upside down. Empty. He tossed it over his shoulder.

"What about you?" Ben asked Blue.

"You'll laugh."

"We want to hear," said Richard.

"Trees."

"Trees?" asked Lou.

"Freedom means I ain't gotta cut no more trees down. Mastah say, 'Blue, go cut down them trees over yonder. See them damned pine trees clutterin' up my view? Get your niggah ass over there and cut 'em down. The hell you doin' sittin' there like a fat bitch dog, Blue? Them trees need choppin'.'" Blue spat in the fire, and held his chin in his hands. "See, I like trees. I like to look at 'em. I like to sit under them and dream. White man see a tree, he think 'Damn, that need cuttin' down.' Me, I don't wanna cut another damned tree down again long as I live."

"What about you, Captain?" Ben asked Richard, who thought for a moment.

"That Shakespeare. He say anything about lions?"

"I suppose so. 'Devouring time, blunt thou the lion's paws, and make the earth devour her own sweet brood.'"

"I'm going home," said Richard, nodding. "I'm going home, and I'm going to kill a certain lion. Or it's gonna kill me, I expect."

"Seems more likely," said Lou. "This world likely kill us all before we make it home."

"And if we ain't got no home?" Blue asked.

"Then I guess you ain't got nothing to lose when you die," said Lou dismissively.

"Guess that's right," said Richard, tossing twigs into the fire. "It's the fighting that counts. You can live in a shit-sty, or you can wipe your bum in a bed of roses, but if you aren't fighting, you're dying."

"Maybe," said Ben after a long pause. "Maybe sometimes you have to know when to start dying."

"The hell is that supposed to mean?" asked Blue, snorting.

"Just...floating downstream isn't always a bad idea. A river doesn't care who wins or loses. Only people do."

"People make my head hurt," said Blue, shaking his head.

"Yes, and trees don't," replied Richard. "Just be careful you don't need one to move out of the way, because you'll break your damned nose when you run into it."

Blue burst into a belly-laugh, tears coming to his eyes.

Richard glanced over to Shenandoah, but she was gone. He noticed an opening between bushes near where she had been sitting.

"What about you, Steps?" Blue asked after his giggles had stopped. "You got a woman?"

"Her name is Talise," Steps replied. "Iroquois."

"How long you been a freeman?"

"Goin' on two years. Know what the best part is? I piss where I want. I'll piss in your garden, or on your horse's leg, or I'll spray it on the moon's face if I feel like it. Ain't nowhere on this dry earth or in that deep black sky up yonder that can hide from me pissin' on it."

Richard stood and stretched as laughter ensued. He quietly made his way between the bushes where he had seen Shenandoah leave, and down an incline through a stand of oak trees. As he moved forward, the voices behind him began to fade.

"I pissed on a goddamned badger once," said Steps.

Hoots broke out.

"I swear! Son of a bitch tried to bite it off. But Steps is too damned quick when he pisses. I piss like the north wind, fast and bold and mean, then I vanish before the last golden drop hits the ground. What your Shakespeare think of that?"

"Think he'd like your poetry..." Ben said.

****

Richard could see clearly, thanks to a brilliant full moon. He placed each step carefully to avoid making a sound. He came to a large hemlock tree and peeked around the trunk, spotting Shenandoah in the distance.

Her knife's handle gripped between her teeth, she lay along a thick oak branch extending about ten feet over a clearing below. The brush kept him from seeing what was beneath her. He held his breath. Like liquid obsidian, her body seemed to flow silently around the branch, and she dropped into the clearing.

A terrible commotion tore through the silence: bleats, snorts, and cracking bushes. Birds launched themselves from their sleeping perches high in the oak tree. A final hoarse death-cry from the deer sounded, and then quiet reigned again.

He moved quickly through the brush and down a small gully, then up again, and crested a tiny hill. As he entered the clearing beneath the giant oak, he saw her sitting with her back to him—her legs folded beneath her, cross-legged, back straight, and her palms open on her knees. Her sparkling skin was covered in sweat. She didn't move or flinch, although he knew she heard him approaching. He stopped just behind her and surveyed the scene. Directly before her lay the dead buck, its throat cut. Dark thick blood pooled in the dirt around its neck and head.

He knelt beside her. She seemed to be in a trance, eyes glazed and staring forward. Her chest, waist, and forearms were blood-spattered, and the blood-stained knife was between her teeth. Her breathing was slow and deep. He reached out and placed his hands on her shoulders. The contact seemed to draw her out of her stupor, and she shivered as she looked in his eyes. Ever so gently, he removed the knife from between her teeth and wiped it on the grass. He hugged her, and she hugged him back as the trembling transformed into a soft weeping.

"Ain't no gods in this land," she said, then reached out and caressed the dead deer's flank. "People don't belong where there's no magic."

He took her head, pressed it against his shoulder, and rocked her. As they moved together, a single firefly flitted near them. Richard watched it dip and weave. More appeared in the clearing, rising from the glistening grass into the air, until they became thousands. They danced an ancient minuet around them.

He removed his coat and placed it around her shoulders, then helped her stand. He heaved the deer up and over his shoulders. They moved toward the lake, not far from the clearing, then stopped to watch the dancing fireflies.

"They're going home," she said.

Richard nodded. "You see? There is magic here."

At the lake, Richard field-dressed the deer with her knife while she washed the blood from herself in the cool water. He helped her dry herself with his coat, then took her in his arms, and they kissed beneath the moon and stars. He wanted more and pressed himself against her belly, but she placed a hand on his chest, looked into his eyes, and shook her head. He once again hoisted the buck across his shoulders, and they made their way toward the waning light of the campfire.

Chapter 8
Butler's Rangers

I t was early morning when Richard and the crew made their way through dense woodland down a narrow path. A musket boomed from the far distance. They froze.

Close to his village, Steps leaped into an awkward sprint toward the sound.

"Steps, wait. Damnit," yelled Richard. He motioned to the others and they followed after Steps.

The path cut up the side of a steep hill. Richard heard men's and women's voices yelling from the top. Two more musket booms echoed. About twenty-five yards in front of them, Steps crested the top of the hill, with Richard and crew close behind.

The village lay before them: ten or twelve huts spread out among the trees at the top of the hill. A large group of women and children huddled together, and four men with tomahawks stood between them and a picket line of Continental Regulars, muskets pointed forward, advancing across a plain a hundred yards in the distance. On their flanks were native fighters.

Steps ran to the four warriors.

"Talise," he called loudly. The men shook their heads and pointed.

Richard and the crew came up and stopped behind them. In front of the advancing troops, where the men had pointed, lay a young native woman face down, a bloody hole in her back.

"Talise!" Steps lunged toward the advancing troops, but the warriors grabbed him by the shoulders and pulled him back. A musket fired and a stump to the left of the men exploded with splinters. Richard and Blue took Steps from the men, and held him tightly.

"No time for this," Richard said to Steps. He shook him. "I am sorry about Talise. Now we fight."

Steps calmed a bit, and they released him. Richard pointed at the women and children. "Shenandoah, get them back behind that berm." He turned to the others. "Deploy behind whatever cover you can find."

One of the native warriors shook his head. "We attack."

"There's too many," Richard replied, his voice rising. Pointing to various vantage points, Richard ordered his crew to settle into a defensive posture.

Shenandoah ran to the women and children. "This way. Move!" She herded them toward the berm behind the village and far back in the opposite direction of the advancing enemy.

Lou and Ben grabbed tomahawks from a boy who offered them, and dropped low behind a ridge of boulders.

Steps settled behind a thick oak tree and loaded his musket. Richard and Blue knelt behind a fallen tree close to Steps as the enemy advanced. Only fifty yards separated them now. Steps pointed at the native warriors deployed on the flanks of the advancing troops.

"Oneida braves," Steps said. "They have pledged their allegiance to the White men who fight the king."

"Where are the rest of your Iroquois men?" Richard asked.

"Off fighting with Colonel Butler, I think."

The four Iroquois warriors raised their voices and shook their tomahawks at the advancing line of troops.

"What the hell are they doing?" asked Richard.

Steps smiled and shook his head. "They will attack."

"They will die."

Steps shrugged and stared at Richard. "But they will die bravely, not hiding behind a tree."

As Richard was about to reply, the four Iroquois braves raised their tomahawks and ran toward the advancing troops, yelling.

"Foolish," Richard said.

"Brave," Steps replied. "They die for their village and families."

Twenty yards from the picket line, muskets barked in unison and the four braves dropped, their bodies tumbling in the grass.

The line of attackers reformed and looked ready to charge. Blue shook his head and leaned close to Richard.

"Too many," Blue said.

"Yup." Then Richard said to Steps, "Stay down when they fire. Wait until you have a clear shot." To Lou and Ben, he called, "Don't show yourself until they're on top of you."

The line of militia fired. Dirt and rocks kicked up in front of Blue and Richard. Bayonets affixed, the attackers charged, the Oneida whooping and hollering. Richard, Steps, and Blue rose, aimed, and fired. Two militiamen dropped to the ground, writhing. The line swept over them as Lou and Ben also stood up. Richard and Steps used their muskets as clubs, and Blue's axe sliced through the air. A militiaman's head rolled on the ground until it stopped upright, eyes blinking, tongue out.

Outnumbered, Richard knew they couldn't last long. He kicked and clubbed a man to a bloody pulp, then sidestepped a bayonet meant to disembowel him.

A soldier headed around the hill that hid the women and children. Richard turned to follow him, but stopped when he saw Shenandoah run straight for the man. At the last moment, when his bayonet was ready to thrust into her chest, she dropped into a ball and rolled, clipping him at the knees. He went sprawling, his musket breaking in half. She sprung up and was on top of him before he could recover. She removed her knife, reached around, and slit his throat.

Richard turned back. An Oneida warrior crashed into his stomach and they fell to the ground, knocking the wind out of him. The warrior pinned him on his back, then raised his tomahawk. Richard tried to twist away. Blue appeared to the side and swung his axe, which sliced into the warrior's shoulder. He dropped the tomahawk and rolled away, screaming. Rising to his feet, he ran into a stand of trees before Richard or Blue could get to him.

Blue helped Richard stand. His legs were rubbery and he struggled to suck air into his lungs. Five soldiers advanced toward them, muskets raised. They paused, as Richard braced himself, and pointed to something behind Blue. He turned to look.

A line of about forty men in green uniforms advanced toward them at a trot, muskets raised and bayonets affixed.

"Rangers," yelled Steps, and shook his musket in the air gleefully. Mixed in with the advancing Rangers were the rest of the village's warriors. Muskets fired, and the attackers dropped or ran. It was over in seconds.

The Rangers surrounded Richard and his crew, their bayonets pointed at them. Richard dropped his musket, and Blue and Steps dropped their weapons as well. Ben and Lou tossed their tomahawks aside and stood, hands raised. Shenandoah approached them, a Ranger guarding her as she walked. The soldiers bound their wrists behind their backs.

Two officers on horseback rode up from behind the hill and reined their horses. Richard recognized one from the tannery: Captain Walter Butler. He removed his hat and dismounted, looking over the crew. He glanced at the dead Oneida and Continental Army bodies that were piled in a heap to the side, their weapons in another pile beside them.

The second officer still on horseback surveyed the village. From his resemblance to the younger man, Richard assumed they were related. It must be Colonel John Butler, he decided. This was where he wanted to be: Butler's Rangers. Not at musket-point, hands tied, however. He chuckled. Blue looked at him strangely and shook his head. None of Richard's crew had been seriously injured.

Captain Butler walked up and studied Richard and his crew. He nodded to a man with sergeant stripes on his arms. "Cut 'em loose."

"Walter, we don't know…" interrupted Colonel Butler.

"They're recruits, Colonel."

Colonel Butler dismounted, stretched, and brushed the dust on his pants off. He nodded to the sergeant, who cut each prisoner's restraints in turn. He walked to Richard and stopped in front of him, sizing him up.

"What's your name, son?"

"Richard Pierpoint. They call me Captain Dick."

Colonel Butler raised an eyebrow. "Do they indeed? I'm Colonel John Butler. This is my son, Captain Walter Butler."

Richard saluted awkwardly. "Sir. I saw your son once. He urged us to come here and fight with you."

Colonel Butler glanced at his son and sighed. "Yes, my son's been very busy recruiting anyone who can walk and skipping out on hangings. I'm hearing that was quite a remarkable thing that you and your men…" He looked down the line, pausing briefly on Shenandoah. "…did here today."

"We ain't his men," said Lou.

Colonel Butler moved to stand in front of Lou. "Your name?"

"Hallelujah. Lou for short."

"Ben Franklin, Colonel. A pleasure to meet you."

The Colonel did a double-take and smiled at Ben.

"Blue-Axe, yer majesty." Several snickers could be heard from the Rangers.

"Just 'Colonel,' if you please," admonished Colonel Butler.

Blue nodded.

The Colonel stepped back and folded his arms.

"What is it exactly you want, gentlemen?" he asked.

"Colonel," Richard began, "Lord Dunmore's proclamation—"

"They want to be Rangers, of course," said Captain Butler.

"Do you mind?" the colonel barked at his son. "The man is speaking."

"I'm sorry, sir." said the Captain.

The colonel nodded to Richard.

"Sir, we can fight, sir. We can be sappers if you want. We just need the chance to prove ourselves."

"Well, son, it appears you held off a raiding party at three-to-one odds. Not too shabby."

"They're mercenaries, Colonel," said Captain Butler, motioning to the pile of dead bodies.

"Yes, Oneida warriors may fight against the king, but they wouldn't attack a village like this." The colonel nodded at the pile of dead militiamen. "And those men aren't from anywhere around here. You got men on that escaped Oneida?" the father asked his son.

"They're tracking him now. He's bleeding, but he got a good head start."

"All right. Give them back their weapons." He motioned for Richard to follow him. "We need to talk."

As Richard, the colonel and the captain turned to walk away, Lou stepped forward.

"Colonel," Lou said loudly.

Colonel Butler stopped and turned to look. "Yes?"

"How come he in charge?"

"Well, Captain Dick. It appears there's a challenge to your authority," said Colonel Butler.

"Damn right there is!" said Lou.

"You think you're the better man?"

"I do."

"I see," replied the colonel and then spoke to his son. "Settle this so there's no doubt among his people, or my troops, as to who is in charge, and bring the man to see me." He turned with a snap and walked toward a large tent that was being erected near the settlement.

Captain Butler picked up a yellow gourd near a thatched hut. He walked about thirty yards away and balanced it on the limb of a tree. He returned to where Richard and Lou stood, drew a straight line in the dirt with the heel of his boot, then stepped back. "Give them each a musket, powder, and three balls, Sergeant Caleb," he said.

The sergeant complied, laying the requested items at Richard's and Lou's feet. The Rangers pushed in closer, the spectacle of a contest beckoning.

"Don't cross that line. First man to knock down that gourd wins. Go!" Butler stepped back and folded his arms.

Lou and Richard regarded each other briefly, then grabbed their muskets.

Lou frantically opened his powder horn and shook the powder down the barrel. Richard hesitated. He looked around, then set his musket back on the ground. He walked three steps behind him and picked up an apple-sized stone. He stepped to the line and hefted it. Lou dropped the ball down the musket barrel and began to pack it as fast as he could.

Richard reached back, eyed the gourd, and let the stone fly. It arced lazily through the air, chipped a small piece off the gourd when it hit, spinning the gourd around until it fell off the branch on the ground. Cheers and laughter broke out.

"That ain't fair. That's cheating!" yelled Lou.

"I never said you had to shoot it down," Captain Butler pointed out.

Lou threw his musket down on the ground and glowered.

"Anybody else want to challenge Captain Dick?"

There were no takers.

Captain Butler stepped in front of Lou, their noses almost touching. Lou flinched, pulling back a step.

"Treat your weapon like that again, and you'll be shoveling donkey shit for the remainder of this war. You understand?"

Lou considered, then unclenched his fists.

"Yes, sir," he replied, not entirely in a respectful tone.

Captain Butler nodded, spun on his heel, and motioned for Richard to follow him.

Ben leaned in close to Blue and whispered, "Well, I think that went spiffy, don't you?"

****

Later that night, the stars hung cold and silent above a rustic lean-to. Beside the fire sat four men. One was Captain Lucius Prescott. The other three were soldiers who wore cruelty and barbarism like a badge. All four reached for their muskets when they heard a rustle. Out of the darkness stumbled an Oneida warrior, his arm a bloody mess from a wicked open wound. One of them raised his musket, but Prescott placed his hand on the barrel and pressed it downward.

"One of ours," said Prescott. The warrior stopped before the fire and dropped to his knees. Prescott squatted beside the exhausted man. "The rest?"

"Only me."

With a deep sigh, Prescott pulled a flask of whiskey from his hip pocket and handed it to the warrior, who drank deeply from it.

"Tell me."

"We attacked. Black warriors surprised us. Then

Rangers came. All dead."

"Except you," pointed out Prescott.

The warrior looked at him, then drank from the flask again.

"Was there a woman with them?"

"Good with a knife."

"That's them," Prescott said and spat into the fire.

"We did as agreed."

"Did you see Butler or his son?"

"No. But there were many Rangers."

"So you want your money."

"We did as agreed," repeated the warrior, sitting back on the ground and coughing.

Prescott had a new riding crop. *Slap, slap, slap* against his thigh it sung. He stood, moved back to his perch in front of the fire.

"Pay him," he said to the man next to him.

The man smiled, reached into his coat and pulled out a small purse. He moved to the warrior and handed it to him. The warrior opened it and looked inside.

In a flash, there was a knife in the man's hand, which he buried deep in the warrior's neck. He fell on his side, legs thrashing, gurgling noises coming from his throat. The men watched in silence as the twisting and convulsions continued.

"Goddamn. How long do I have to watch this?" Prescott asked. He stood, strode to the writhing man, and twisted the knife up and to the left. The thrashing stopped as the warrior finally quieted and died. "Next time, stick it in the goddamn artery, not the larynx. Now haul it down to the river and get rid of it," he said, wiping his hand on one of the men's shirt.

"How come I gotta—"

"You kill it, you clean it up."

The man cursed, grabbed the ankles of the dead Oneida warrior, and lugged the body toward the river in the distance.

"We break camp now," Prescott said to the other men. "Let's move out."

****

In a tent lit by several lanterns, Richard and Colonel Butler hovered over a large map spread on a table. The Colonel's son sat on a stool in the corner, an ankle crossed over a knee.

"These denote Loyalist homesteads," Colonel Butler said, marking off three locations on the map. "They're off limits. You may call on them for help in an emergency, but don't push it. Most wish to keep their anonymity."

Richard nodded. "And all the rest are Patriot, or leaning Patriot."

"Yes, correct. Your contact and commanding officer will be my son, Captain Butler. I need information on any troop movements or other activity involving more than five or six people."

"Where will we be based?"

"That's up to you. I wouldn't stay anywhere longer than a few days. Meet here on the first of the month for provisions," the colonel said, stepping back from the map.

"That's it?"

"No. Harass the enemy. They're traitors, after all. Burn their supplies. Confiscate or destroy their property. Kill them if they resist."

"Slaves are considered property."

"As I said, confiscate their property," Colonel Butler said slowly, emphasizing each word.

Captain Butler rose from his seat and stood next to Richard. "We want you to be the biggest goddamned gadfly to ever bite a horse's ass," the captain said. "The colonel doesn't think you can handle it."

"Am I mistaken, son?" asked the colonel.

"Sir, I imagine you are never mistaken. Only occasionally misinformed," answered Richard with a curt bow.

Colonel Butler laughed and slapped his son on the back.

"A goddamned diplomat and warrior rolled into one," said the Colonel.

"So it seems," said Captain Butler with a smile.

Captain Butler rolled up the map and handed it to Richard, who turned to leave.

"By the way," Captain Butler called to him. "You must still survive basic training. You and your crew are to report to Sergeant Caleb at dawn tomorrow."

"And Captain Dick?" said the colonel. "If you get caught, none of you will fare well."

"I know, sir."

Richard saluted. As he left the tent, he heard the two men's voices faintly from inside.

"I hope you're right. I've never known a Negro to be a fighter," said Colonel Butler.

"We shall see, won't we?"

Chapter 9
Beautiful Daughter of the Stars

S henandoah sat on the thick branch of an oak tree in the late afternoon, her back braced against its massive trunk, and whittled furiously. A group of Iroquois and Rangers, as well as Blue, Lou, Ben, and Steps, were gathered below her at a makeshift finish line, waiting for the contestants to arrive. The foot-race was organized and thought up by the sadistic Sergeant Caleb. One person had been nominated from the Rangers, one warrior from the Iroquois, and one man from "Captain Dick's Raggedy Entourage," as Caleb had called it. Richard was chosen, of course.

Sergeant Caleb was built like a bull with practically no neck. His hairless dome sat atop massive shoulders like a watermelon, and tree-trunk arms tapered to massive, calloused hands. He rarely wore a shirt, his skin tanned to a deep umber.

They'd risen early with the sun. Shavings from Shenandoah's whittled stick flew in all directions as she remembered being told that, being a woman, she wasn't allowed to be part of the training. She'd expected that, but not Richard's meek and sheep-like acquiescence to the ban. She knew he had no control over it, but it still irked her, and she'd taken her pique out on him, ignoring him when he'd spoken to her, shaking off his hand when he'd placed it on her shoulder and tried to "explain" things.

"They're about to start. Best git," she'd said dismissively and turned away, the anger seething beneath her surface of apparent unconcern. He'd walked away, shaking his head. She'd thought about picking up a rock and throwing it at his head, but then laughed under her breath.

"*Control your anger, child,*" her mother's voice repeated in her head. "*No control will get you killed. Control will let you do the killin', baby.*"

She had taken a deep breath, determined to watch everything that happened during the training, to absorb it, memorize it, learn from their failures, visualize herself making each movement with her own muscles over and over again.

She and her mother had been taken by slavers when she was five years old. She remembered little of it—had lost the memories deliberately, she supposed. They were brought to America on a ship with fifty or more others, and then sold at auction in South Carolina. Though they were kept together, they were given new names: mother Canna, and daughter Bono.

She tossed the whittled nub away, all that was left of the stick, and contemplated the gleaming tip of her knife. Her mother had been thirty-five years old when she died. Shenandoah remembered it as sharply as the pointy end of the weapon that appeared in front of her eyes.

Her mother had been assigned as a house slave after five years of back-breaking labor in the fields had bent her spine.

One day, the owner's seventeen-year-old son had gotten drunk at a family gathering and boasted that Shenandoah's mother had tried to seduce him, had cornered him in the barn, and had her way with him. If her mother had accepted his story, or even kept silent, she might still be alive. But she told the truth, that the boy was a liar, that he'd raped her at knife-point and cut her on her buttocks. She even showed the still-healing scar to the owner and his wife.

They took her out to the field, called every slave to watch, drove four stakes in the ground and tied her naked and spread-eagled, on her back. Then they whipped her breasts, stomach, and loins with a bullwhip, until red welts appeared everywhere, and the blood dripped down her ribcage and inner thighs long after her strangled screams had turned to a low growl of death. Her heart had exploded from the strain. Shenandoah believed that to be true, believed it was her mother's heart that gave out.

They buried her behind nigger-hill, in a shallow grave with no marker, among the other nameless slaves they'd used up and discarded.

Years later, when Shenandoah had reached the age of maturity, the owner himself had turned his attention to her.

It was in the wee hours of the night that she ran. Only Hallelujah had seen her go, had given her a wineskin of water and a knife.

"I ain't ready yet," he had said. "Go north, sleep during the day, travel at night. Chances are you're gonna be raped or killed or resold. Kill yourself first if possible, or at least take as many down as you can. Now run, woman. Like the goddamn wind."

"My name is Shenandoah," she replied. An old Algonquin woman who had worked as a cook on the plantation had told her it meant *beautiful daughter of the stars.* "And I'm going home, Lou."

He'd slammed his fist, without much heart behind it, against the doorjamb, then turned and shut the door to the slave quarters behind him.

****

Shenandoah glanced up at the low-hanging sun as rusty shadows dusted the tips of the blue spruce trees encircling the settlement and camp. There was still no sign of Richard or the other the two men, who were racing through the forest for the finish line. She closed her eyes and replayed the day's lessons, letting them seep into her mind and muscles.

After the camp had retired, she would sneak out under the moon and stars, take a musket, and practice loading and reloading. Most of the men were catching on, except perhaps for Ben, who had the hardest time physically of all of them.

Tomorrow was the day they became Rangers.

She had watched as the men fired at targets on a makeshift range. Behind them, Sergeant Caleb had stalked, watching every move. When he'd yell the command to fire and only half of the muskets ignited, it would drive him crazy.

"Shite! Fucking shite, girls. Again. Load, load, load." He'd hovered above their heads, screaming in their ears. "Any goddamned day now. Start again. Lord God Almighty has postponed bloody judgment day waiting for you ladies."

She noticed that Caleb had settled, for some reason, on Ben as his favorite object of attention. He barked hoarse commands in Ben's ear as his fingers shook, fumbling with the powder horn which would invariably end up on the ground spilling its contents.

"What a clutch of bloody damned tomnoddies! Finesse. Concentrate. Don't look at me, boy, look at what you're about."

****

There was a commotion below her, a murmuring in the

crowd. She looked back up and, from her vantage point in the tree, saw movement about a hundred yards in the distance. Richard appeared atop a small hill. On his naked back, he carried the four-foot thick log that he'd started the race with. About thirty feet behind him appeared the Ranger, hefting his own log. He was a hairy man who seemed to be all muscle and gristle. The Iroquois warrior trudged close behind him, and a gauntlet line of Rangers formed near the finish line.

The path in front of Richard had been blocked, deliberately, by a large fallen tree. Shenandoah stood up on the limb so she could get a better view. As he stopped before the tree, she could see sweat plastered his body, and blood dripped down his back from where the bark of the log he carried had cut and chafed into his shoulders. He took the log, balanced it on end, heaved it up and over the tree trunk with a loud grunt, then scrambled over it just as the Ranger and the native warrior caught up to him.

Richard grabbed the log, hoisted it again to his torn shoulders, chest pumping like a bellows, and stumbled toward the gauntlet and finish line. Shenandoah noticed Captain Butler step outside his tent and fold his arms, watching the spectacle.

She dropped silently to the ground and moved quickly to the crude line dug in the sand. Richard made his way straight toward her, his eyes focused, and the Ranger was now over the fallen tree and not far behind. As Richard entered the gauntlet, the troops jeered and hooted, flung insults at him, and screamed obscenities.

As he stumbled forward, about ten feet from the finish line, Sergeant Caleb stuck his leg out and tripped Richard, who fell face forward into the dust, his log rolling a few feet away.

Richard looked up at him.

"We don't let girls join the King's Rangers," yelled the sergeant. "Only men. Which is it? You a girl or a man? Or be you something in between?"

Richard growled between his clenched teeth, pushed himself to his feet, grabbed the end of the log, dragging it behind him, and lurched over the finish line only seconds before the Ranger and the Iroquois warrior arrived with their logs.

A cheer rose from all the men. Shenandoah screamed and danced with Blue and Ben, the three holding hands. Sergeant Caleb shook his head with a grin and spat into the dust.

"You're a bloody mess, Ranger," Caleb said to Richard, holding his hand out.

Richard grinned and took it. As he stood and embraced Shenandoah, she looked toward Butler's tent, but he was gone.

****

In the darkness of their lean-to shelter, she gently rubbed sunflower oil into Richard's back and shoulders. The bleeding had stopped, leaving raw grooves in his flesh that were swollen and ugly. She sat on his lower back, admiring the slope and curve as it narrowed toward his waist. She gently dragged her nails over the back of his arms, then down the sides of his rib cage. He shivered as she leaned in and kissed the back of his neck. The rumble of thunder washed over them.

The tip of her tongue curled around the inside of his ear.

"I want a musket, too."

He tensed. "You can't be a Ranger, Shenandoah," he murmured. He tried to kiss her.

She pushed him away, stood up, and stepped outside their shelter. He rose up on his elbows and looked at her. Rain began to fall.

"Says you," she said, putting her hands on her hips.

He sighed as her eyes flashed. "Says the king."

She stepped closer and leaned toward him. Raindrops spattered off her forehead and the water ran off her chin in rivulets. Lightning flashed.

"Damn your king. I'm going to fight for my freedom and for others like that little girl in the barn. Try to stop me, Captain Dick. You just try," she said.

She furrowed her brow and jutted her jaw forward.

He reached toward her. "Come inside. You're getting soaked." He flinched when her response was a violent flick of her head which sent droplets of water spraying in all directions. She pointed a finger at him and wagged it. She could feel her mother's spirit rising in her.

"You can sleep by your damn self." As she stomped off into the darkness, she heard him calling out to her, but she kept her eyes focused forward, the pelting rain plastering her hair to her face. A peal of thunder cracked simultaneously with the white flash of a nearby lightning strike.

She stopped, looked up into the sky, and opened her mouth to taste the cool, sweet water that fell.

Control will let you do the killin', she heard her mother say. Slowly, second by second, she brought her heaving chest to bay, smoothed out each shallow breath until it was steady and deep.

A line of lean-to shelters for the men ran along before her. She stepped inside the nearest lean-to about thirty yards away below a tall spruce. Facing in opposite directions slept Blue and Ben. She shook the water from herself as best she could and snuggled between the backs of the two men.

Blue farted, causing her to giggle, and he began to snore. Ben looked over his shoulder at her, an eyebrow raised in surprise. He opened his mouth to say something but was interrupted by another deep rumble from Blue's behind. He glanced at Blue, then shook his head.

"You have no idea how bad it is, Madam." He pulled his blanket up and covered her with it.

She snuggled in closer to his back for warmth.

"Good night, Shenandoah."

"Good night, Ben Franklin."

****

Richard's crew stood in line in front of the quartermaster wagon. Shenandoah stood to the side, arms folded, watching. Her legs crossed, she leaned back against a hemlock tree.

First Lou and Steps received their uniform after a quick fitting, and then each received a new musket and paraphernalia, backpack, bedroll, cup, and knife. Then Ben and Blue stepped forward. It took four tries to find a uniform to fit Blue, but they managed somehow.

As Richard came forward, he looked towards her. He opened his mouth, but she looked away, keeping her face hard and cold.

When she looked back, the quartermaster handed Richard a musket. He hefted it and said "I want two."

She stared at him, surprised, and he stared back at her.

"One per soldier," said the quartermaster, folding his

arms.

"I want two," repeated Richard defiantly, turning back to the quartermaster.

Sergeant Caleb, who had been watching, stepped forward. He looked at Shenandoah, and she returned his gaze, not breaking eye contact until he smiled. He turned to the quartermaster.

"Give him two," said Sergeant Caleb.

"Sergeant, you know the regs."

"Give this Ranger another goddamned weapon," he screamed in the quartermaster's face.

Red-faced, the quartermaster turned, grabbed another musket with powder horn and shot, and shoved it out to Richard. He took it, walked to Shenandoah, and held it out to her.

She took a deep breath, and relaxed the firm control of her face muscles. She reached out and took it from him.

"I'm sorry if I…" he began, but she turned on her heel and walked away.

As she walked, part of her knew it wasn't what she wanted to do, she had wanted to kiss him and thank him, to accept his apology. Still, she'd gotten what she wanted from him. She had a musket now like all the men, and no one was going to take away her dignity like they'd taken her mother's.

Chapter 10

Boyle's Heaven

O ralee stood at the kitchen window and watched her grandchildren—Elijah, the younger at thirteen, and Marcus, fifteen—haul heavy sacks of grain on their backs from the barn to a horse-drawn cart. They wore short burlap pants and floppy shoes. It was brutally hot, and the air was heavy with a wicked humidity. She wiped her face with a towel and shook her head. Just standing in the kitchen, her homespun hemp and flax dress hung on her like a soaked rag, and it itched and chafed. The boys were strong, but in this heat she worried about them.

Their mother, Oralee's daughter, had died two years ago this spring, after their master's wife had died from an infection in her teeth. Oralee shuddered at the memory.

Bad way to leave this world.

Their mother's death had been rough on both boys, although Elijah took it the hardest. He had acted out twice this year by breaking some heirloom plates deliberately, both times getting a harsh whipping. She could see the scars on his sweaty back, which had only recently begun to heal, as he tossed another fat sack on the pile.

Oralee's master, Shadrach Boyle, had never whipped any of his slaves prior to his own wife's death, and it almost seemed to Oralee that he'd lost a part of his soul when she died. His cruelty had grown with his bitterness. Often, he'd fly into a rage, screaming obscenities at no one in particular, his face purple and his lips spraying spittle on the floor. Then he'd drop to his knees and weep, calling out for Oralee. His apologies made her uncomfortable, for he'd cling to her leg, his chest heaving, tears falling on the scrubbed wooden floor.

Perhaps it was the deep pool of guilt that had dripped into his heart over the years, the pain and self-disgust from owning other human beings, which caused him to interpret his own wife's agonizing death as God's judgement and punishment. Whatever it was, he'd legalized her own, the boys', and her uncle Venture's freedom. *Emancipation*, she repeated the long word in her mind. He'd also shown her his legal will, giving his land and property to her and the boys upon his death. She didn't hate the man, but she didn't feel sorry for him either, at least not most of the time.

She glanced at a drawing of her daughter, the boys' mother, that Marcus had made on a torn piece of parchment and which hung over the stove. She missed Coffey terribly. Her daughter's arm had been severed by a plow blade that fell from a rusty hook in the barn rafters, and she'd bled to death. Two years gone now, so close to freedom, so close to her dreams.

Oralee sighed and wiped her face again with the towel. There was no way she was going to light a fire in the stove for dinner, so she needed to go down in the cellar and get some pickled beets and salted fish for dinner.

Picking up a small basket of eggs on the kitchen counter, she stepped outside and walked toward the cellar doors. Venture, her uncle, worked to repair a broken wagon between the barn and corral of ten milk cows.

Venture hardly spoke lately, and sometimes forgot his own name. His hair was white, his face leathery and cracked. He rarely ate, and his bones seemed about to poke through his skin. Oralee had tried to spoon porridge down his throat while he slept. He'd only choked on it and spat it out. He seemed to be surviving on water alone as of late.

"Y'all get outta the sun now, Venture," she called to him. "That wagon can wait until morning."

He turned when she called out to him and waved. Sometimes he'd stare at her as if she were a stranger. Today, his wide smile deepened the creases in his face, and his eyes conveyed recognition. He shrugged and went back to work with his file. She sighed, pulled the durag from her head and wrung it out, then put it back on. Her large frame and the extra weight she had put on over the past year made summer a difficult time for her.

As she came around the side of the house, she spotted Shadrach in the distance standing a few feet from the horse and cart. He was talking and laughing with a uniformed man who watched the boys load it with grain. She opened the door and descended the steep steps to the darkened cellar. The coolness made her sigh in relief. She sat on top of the barrel of dried fish and leaned her head against the damp dirt behind her, closing her eyes, holding the eggs in her lap. Cracks in the cellar door above filtered yellow threads of light into the gloomy interior.

She knew what was going on with the grain that the boys were loading into the wagon. In the evenings, Shadrach used to play cards with his wife, Jessica, in candlelight, while Oralee would do her knitting. He'd either read from the Bible or talk about the fact the other farmers in the area were all Loyalists, and Shadrach would curse them, and then expound for hours about the evils of monarchy. She knew he was supplying the revolutionaries, as he called them, with staples like grain, and that it was a dangerous business called treason.

Sighing, she took one of the smaller eggs from the basket and set it on the floor beside her foot, then waited. From behind a bag of grain, Nachash appeared and slithered on the floor toward her. A six-foot-long corn-snake, Nachash's orange and ruby scales were covered with variegated black lines that crossed its back in a regular pattern. The snake curled up beside her ankle, touching her for warmth. It unhinged its jaw and began to swallow the egg whole.

The snake suddenly backed up, closed its mouth, and slithered back to its hiding place, leaving the egg. Oralee frowned and looked to her left into the darkened corner of the cellar. She squinted and saw the outline of a face. The outline became a real face, the face of her Coffey. Curly locks, long thin face, wide nose, high cheekbones, full lips.

"Coffey." Her lips trembled as she whispered her daughter's name, and sweat beaded on her forehead. She pressed her back as hard as she could against the soft, damp walls of the cellar. At that moment, a heavy cloud must have come across the face of the sun, for the meager light was doused, and she was drenched in total darkness.

She held her breath, listening. She could hear the faint inhale and exhale of someone breathing slowly, calmly, from not too far away.

The light returned, and a Black woman stood no more than ten feet from Oralee. The resemblance to Coffey was remarkable, but it definitely wasn't her. Oralee let her breath out and wiped her eyes.

"I didn't mean to scare you, ma'am. I'm sorry I'm not Coffey. My name is Shenandoah." Her voice was low, breathy, and her eyes were soft. Yet in her hand she held a musket pointed at the ground, and strapped to her leg was a large knife in a sheath. She wore moccasins, deerskin pants, and her shirt looked to be a man's, with a wide collar and the top buttons open to reveal a well-defined musculature in her neck and shoulders. Her clothing was well-worn, and it appeared to fit her with such a relaxed and natural perfection, it almost seemed to Oralee that she could have been born wearing the outfit while it grew in size as she did.

"I'm...I'm Oralee." The woman didn't seem dangerous despite the gun and the wicked blade on her thigh. "What you want here?"

Shenandoah leaned her musket against the wall and knelt at Oralee's feet. She picked up the egg and handed it to her. "No more snakes gonna take your food," she said with a soft smile.

****

Richard squinted as he stared through the telescopic eyepiece. He lay on his stomach on a grassy knoll about two hundred yards from the farm. His crew knelt behind him, except for Shenandoah, whom he'd sent around the back of the property to scout and to see if she could make contact with the slaves.

At the entrance to the farm, a crudely hung sign read "Shadrach Boyle's Heaven." An older man with a short beard and bald head, who appeared to be the owner, stood below the sign next to a Continental soldier and a wagon full of grain. Two young Black boys who had been loading it ran to an old man who was fixing a broken wheel beside the barn. Richard slid down the backside of the knoll toward his men.

"You two take the wagon," Richard said, motioning to Ben and Blue. "Scare him off and burn it."

"But what if——" began Ben.

"Don't want anybody hurt, but you do what you gotta do, even if that means somebody gets hurt."

The two men nodded, then scrambled the rest of the way down the hill. Richard returned to the top and watched as the two men shook hands. Then the soldier climbed into the horse-drawn wagon and drove it toward the road. The owner turned and walked back into the house.

Richard motioned for Steps and Lou to join him at the crest. He noticed movement and trained his scope on the doors of a cellar on the side of the house. A female slave climbed out and called to the boys and old man. From his vantage point, he could just make out her voice.

"Elijah, Marcus, you bring Venture and come in the house right now, you hear me?" she yelled.

The two boys tried to pull the old man by his sleeve, but he pulled back and shooed them away. They ran toward the woman, who herded them into the back door of the house. Once they were inside, Shenandoah exited the cellar, then motioned to Richard that she was going around the back side of the house as well. Richard waved back then leaned toward Lou and pointed.

"You go around the back with her. Nobody comes out. You hear any shooting out front, you go inside and make sure the woman and those children are safe."

Lou gave a curt nod and sprinted toward the direction Richard had pointed.

"Let's do this. Hopefully, it'll be easy," Richard said,

turning to Steps.

Steps raised an eyebrow as the two men walked directly toward the front door of the house. They stopped about twenty feet from the porch.

"Shadrach Boyle! Come out!" yelled Richard.

A curtain pulled aside from a window beside the door as Shadrach Boyle stared out at the two Black Rangers. His eyes went wide, and he pulled the curtain tight.

****

Oralee stood in the kitchen, hugging her grandchildren to herself. Shadrach was in the front room. She heard the soldier call for her master from the front of the house.

"Oralee!" yelled Shadrach. He ran into the kitchen. "They're your people. What the hell do they want? Negro British soldiers—ain't never seen nothing like that in my life."

Shadrach was a thin, wiry man with a bald head. In his quivering right hand he held an old, dull machete that used to hang on the wall in the main room. When she didn't answer, but only shook her head, he ran back into the front room. She peeked around the corner.

Shadrach leaned against the door jamb and opened the door a crack, peeking out.

"The hell you want?" Shadrach yelled.

"Come outside, Boyle. We gotta talk," the Black soldier yelled back.

Shadrach stuck his machete out the door and waved it around. "You ain't welcome here. Go away!"

"You been supplying goods to damn traitors. We're confiscating your property in the name of the Crown," replied the Black man who seemed to be in charge.

"What? You bastards are seriously mucked in the head. Get the hell off my land!"

"We ain't got all day. You got twenty seconds," replied the soldier.

Shadrach slammed the door and slid down to a sitting position, his back against the wall. Oralee pulled her wide-eyed grandchildren back in the kitchen with her. She glanced out the kitchen window and saw Shenandoah watching her, with another soldier beside her. She motioned for Oralee to get down.

Oralee sat down on the floor beside the cupboards, pulling Marcus and Elijah with her.

****

As Richard and Steps waited for Shadrach's decision, Richard watched Blue and Ben walk up the drive.

"Well?" Richard asked as they stopped beside him.

"Ran the wagon into a swamp over yonder. Set the horse loose," Blue said.

"The soldier?"

Blue grinned and held up a pair of pants. "Walking back to town without his breeches."

Richard laughed, then sighed. "Time to finish this." He turned to the house, cupped his hand beside his mouth, and yelled. "Time's up, Shadrach. You coming out or are we coming in?"

The group waited in silence for several seconds. Richard glanced to the barn and saw the old man watching them. He smiled and waved at Richard. Richard waved back.

The door burst open. Shadrach flew out, screaming obscenities, his machete raised above his head. Steps aimed his musket, but Richard stepped in and pressed the barrel down.

"We can handle him."

As Shadrach closed on Richard, his face contorted, a *boom* came from the side of the house. The left half of Shadrach's head exploded. He collapsed, and his machete tumbled to Richard's feet.

"Good shooting!" yelled the old man beside the barn, clapping his hands. Ten feet from him stood Hallelujah with a smoking musket.

Blue shook his head. "Guess that's the end of that."

Shenandoah stepped from the front door of the house. "All clear," she called and went back inside.

Ben whistled. "How bloody damned invigorating a soldier's life is! The stories I'll be able to tell…"

Richard glared at Lou, who shrugged, a smirk on his face, and lowered his weapon.

Richard walked into the kitchen with Shenandoah behind him. The woman he had seen stood near a counter, the two boys behind her. She held a large knife in her hand.

"You can put that down," Richard said, his hand extended.

"Her name's Oralee," Shenandoah prompted him.

Oralee glanced at Shenandoah, who smiled and nodded her head. Oralee set the knife on the counter behind her.

Her eyes narrowed. "What you want? Who are you?"

"You can call me Captain Dick. We shot him. It's okay now."

"What you mean it's okay?"

"You're free," he answered, smiling.

"Of course we're free. We been free."

"I mean you're free. You can go now. You ain't got no master."

Oralee stared at him. "You ain't hearing me," she said and folded her arms. "Where we gonna go? We got a roof over our heads, a bed to sleep in, food, firewood, good water."

Richard regarded her with a quizzical look. "But-"

"Got kids. Got old folks. We ain't young bucks like you."

"You'd rather be a slave?"

A scowl came across Oralee's face. She pointed her finger at Richard. "Don't you put words in Oralee's mouth. I'd rather be alive. You gonna take care of all of us? Feed us? Find us a home?"

He stared at her, his fists clenched. Sighing deeply, he sat on a small stool behind him. His shoulders slumped. "Well damn. This isn't the way it's supposed to go."

Her face softened. She walked up and put her hand on Richard's shoulder. "All y'all have dinner with us tonight."

****

They sat around the dining table as Oralee and her boys served them dinner. Corn, potatoes, and salted herring. Each member of the crew had a heaping plate of food placed in front of them. The last to be served was Richard. Oralee exited the kitchen and set a plate of nothing but red roses in front of him. She stepped back and waited for his reaction, an eyebrow raised.

Richard frowned, then shook his head and nodded. He understood.

Oralee was relieved. "We're grateful, son," she said. "But sometimes ideas like freedom are pretty flowers. Nice to look at and smell, they even make your heart sing, but it's the corn and potatoes that keep us alive. Potatoes first, then the roses."

Chapter 11
Autumn Cider

R ichard led the crew through a narrow path in the woods. Behind them was a line of twenty newly freed slaves, including four children. The children laughed, chased butterflies and sang songs. Shenandoah stepped up and shushed them.

It had been over a year since their misadventure with Shadrach Boyle and Oralee, and their clothes already hung on them like old rags, scuffed and torn in places. The men had begun to grow beards that made them look menacing, and Shenandoah's hair was so long she tied it in a tight ponytail. They came to a crossroad where someone had nailed a poster to a tall maple tree. Blue ran up, examined it, pulled a bit of charcoal from his knapsack, and drew something on it. The crew gathered around to look.

"WANTED: CAPTAIN DICK - For Treason and Sundry Acts of Treachery - REWARD!"

Beneath the caption was a figure of an angry, wild-eyed Black man in a Ranger's uniform carrying a musket. Blue had drawn an oversized, crude approximation of a male member on the figure.

Richard examined it, then nodded. "That'll do."

After a trek of nearly a mile, they came to a clearing with about thirty tents made of gray canvas pitched in a circle, and a large group of freed slaves—mostly women and children—mingling in the sunshine. In the center of the circle was a large fire pit where many women were busy repairing worn-out uniforms for the soldiers.

Five or six Rangers camped nearby. Male former slaves were already with Butler, training to become Rangers. Richard was aware that they were taking the women and children to permanent shelters, provided by the British government, for the coming winter north of the Niagara River in Ontario.

****

Richard sat in cool water near the shore of a small lake not far from the encampment. He washed himself with a bar of real soap—a true luxury. About twenty feet behind him, Lou scrubbed his grimy skin in the lake water.

The two men had hardly spoken lately. Lou had become sullen and taciturn, grumbling at every inconvenience. When confronted with Richard's displeasure that Lou had shot Shadrach Boyle, it had nearly ended in fisticuffs. From that point forward, Lou had retreated from poking at everything Richard did, and an uneasy truce had held.

Richard lathered his head with the soap, digging into his scalp with his fingernails, the sensation exquisite. He dipped below the water, and when he rose and wiped his eyes, he saw Shenandoah in the far distance also approach the shoreline. Apparently unaware of the two men watching her, she removed her clothes and stepped into the water.

"That's a sight. No offense, Captain," Lou said.

"None taken," Richard replied, without turning to look at him. Shenandoah's casual relationship with her own body, with nudity, was something he was only lately getting used to. It almost seemed sometimes like she didn't care what others thought, that she was standing outside the box that others had built for themselves and for the world to be confined by.

Shenandoah swam out into the lake, then turned on her back to float, her breasts outlined by the water. The two men stared for several minutes.

"So…she ever tell you who else she's been with?" asked Lou.

"Nope. And I never asked."

"Ever wonder?"

"Nope."

"Me, I'd be interested."

Richard stood, finally, and faced Lou directly. "Thankfully, I ain't you. Because if I was, I'd expect to get my teeth knocked out if I kept running my jaw like that."

Lou stood up as well, and the two men faced each other.

"That a threat?" Lou asked with a sneer. "You being a captain and all, I suppose I should be shaking."

"Nope. Just an observation of the facts."

Lou gestured toward Shenandoah, who still floated face-up far out on the lake. "Only fact I know for sure is that is a sweet little tinder box."

Richard closed his eyes briefly, took a deep breath, then opened them. "Now I know that's intended to provoke me. But it don't. I don't give a damn who she was with, even if it was someone like you. You want to know what does provoke me?"

"What's that?"

"A man that needs to use a woman in order to poke at another man. You want to poke at me, poke away. But next time you bring her into whatever problem you got with me, it ain't gonna go well for you. There's a threat for you." Richard turned away and walked onto the shore. He pulled his pants on, his back to Lou.

Lou stood with his arms folded and grinned. "Here's some advice for you, Captain. She like it down on all fours. Just like a dog."

Richard stopped and, with only his breeches on, he turned and walked back into the water straight for Lou. Lou unfolded his arms and began to backtrack. Dipping his shoulder down, Richard lunged forward and drove straight into Lou's midsection. Both men tumbled into the water, their arms flailing. Richard held Lou's head below the waterline briefly, but a flying fist against his temple knocked him to the side and into the water. They reached for each other and grappled, pulling and pushing, the water making them feel heavy and slow.

Blue, Ben, and Steps ran over the hill and pulled both men apart. They dragged a swinging Richard away and out of the water. Lou knelt in the water, his chest heaving. His nose dripped blood.

Pulling Richard by the arms, the three men dragged him up the hill as Shenandoah stood in the distance watching, already fully clothed. As he crested the hill, the men released him. He turned and regarded Lou.

"Y'ain't no goddamned captain!" Lou screamed. "You ain't nobody. Just another bloody nigger slave like the rest of us pretending they free. Hear me? Nobody!"

Shenandoah stared at Lou, then turned, expressionless, and made her way toward Richard and the men on the hill.

****

Richard and Shenandoah lay on their backs beneath their lean-to, under a blanket, their heads out, gazing at the stars. The heavens blazed above them, resplendent.

Leaning up on one elbow, she reached over and caressed his bearded chin. "You don't have to protect me from him."

He looked at her and shook his head. When he opened his mouth to speak, she put two fingers to his lips and smiled impishly. She leaned in close to his ear, her breath warm and soft, and whispered, "I am your woman."

She climbed on top, straddling him. She nestled her head gently against his and began to press and roll her hips. Her hair smelled of sweet pea, spicy and green. When he kissed her, her lips tasted like maple candy, mixed with a hint of cinnamon. He ran his fingers down her back, causing her to shiver, and held her hips as she continued to undulate. He opened his eyes and stared at the endless sky.

They were encircled by tall trees wearing plumes of orange and ruby, as if licked by autumn's fiery tongue. He looked up past her shoulder.

The universe shifted, and the stars suddenly seemed to be below them. They floated above the expanse like gods, intimately connected. He held her tightly to him, afraid she might fall out of his arms into the sea of stars below. Her breath merged with his, and their heartbeats became one, her breasts pressed tightly to him.

Their love-making was sweet and rich, like autumn cider.

When their breathing slowed, the call of a loon on the distant lake echoed through the trees as their commingled sweat cooled them in the fall night air.

"Are we closer to home?" she asked.

"Every day," he whispered and believed it.

Soon, he slept, and once again he dreamed of lions.

Chapter 12
Valley Forge

Lieutenant-Colonel John Laurens of the Continental Army rode in the chilly rain. Wrapped in a white canvas over his new blue uniform, he hunched in the saddle to avoid the pelting rain. His horse neighed, then shook its mane, causing it to stumble. Once righted, they continued on the road toward the small guardhouse near the entrance to General George Washington's, and the Continental Army's, winter encampment, Valley Forge.

Laurens was a young man of twenty-three. With a high forehead and handsome face, he was a man of studious intellect and ambitious ideals. He'd only recently joined the Army as an aide-de-camp to the general after begging his father, Henry Laurens of South Carolina and the current President of Congress, for permission to leave England, where Laurens was studying law, and return to fight as a soldier.

The two guards checked his papers quickly, then waved him on, eager to return to the comfort of the guardhouse. He rounded a bend, and before him, Washington's encampment spread out in a sea of tents. The army of twelve thousand men had lost the city of Philadelphia to British forces and stumbled back in disarray to Valley Forge in Pennsylvania near the Schuylkill River.

Laurens rode to a two-story stone and mortar home—the army's current headquarters—dismounted, and tied off his horse. Officers of different rank entered and exited, hunched over against the pelting rain. Pushing through the door, he shook off his canvas cloak and hung it on a hook. The room was filled with men who talked excitedly in small groups beside a huge map pinned to a wall.

A man in the far corner, dressed meticulously in the uniform of a French general, noticed him and waved him over. Laurens smiled and pushed through the throng of half-soaked officers. The Marquis de Lafayette held out a wine glass filled with a deep red claret to Laurens. Laurens took the wine gratefully and downed it in one gulp, much to the amusement of Lafayette.

"Colonel Laurens, welcome to Valley Shite-hole."

Laurens held out his hand. "General Lafayette."

The general would have none of it, and embraced Laurens.

Lafayette refilled Laurens's glass. "Tell me, John, how is your father?"

"They made him President of Congress." Laurens sipped and savored the wine now, appreciating its deep complexity. It was definitely a French vintage.

"Did they? Then he is in the ninth circle of hell. I shall pray for him."

Laurens laughed and looked around at the bustle of activity, the raised voices, and men shaking hands.

Lafayette followed his gaze. "Ah. You haven't heard."

"Heard?"

"General Clinton has abandoned Philadelphia. They scurry back to New York like vermin."

Laurens's eyes widened. "Then France has declared for us!"

"So we have. This army prepares to march on the

morrow to retake the city, and not a moment too soon. I would rather be dragged naked through the streets of that English cesspool, London, than stay another day on this blasted piece of ground. *Merde!*"

Laurens chuckled. "Is he in?"

"He is expecting you." Lafayette leaned in close, his brow furrowed with concern. "Pray, a word of advice?"

"Of course."

"This campaign has taken its toll. Tread lightly or not at all."

Laurens nodded and handed Lafayette his empty wine glass. Lafayette stepped back and bowed. Laurens returned the bow, relinquished his sword to a guard near the stairs to the second floor, and ascended. Once at the top, he knocked and waited.

"Enter," a deep voice said.

He opened the door and went inside. George Washington sat in a wing-back chair beside a roaring fireplace, holding an open book. A red blanket covered his lap and legs, which were extended and crossed, propped on an ottoman. He wore a white shirt open at the collar, a pair of reading glasses squatting on the tip of his prominent nose. Unlike most other gentlemen who removed their wigs in privacy, Washington never wore a wig. He powdered, curled, and tied his own long hair in a queue at the nape of his neck.

Billy Lee, Washington's Black personal valet, sat on a stool in the corner, polishing a pair of boots. There was a table in the center of the room with a huge map spread across the top.

"General Washington, sir." Laurens snapped to attention and saluted. "Lieutenant-Colonel John Laurens."

"John!" Washington removed his reading glasses, stood, and dropped the blanket on the chair behind him. "So good to see you. At ease." The general extended his hand.

Relaxing, Laurens took Washington's hand.

"Please have a seat. Would you like some tea?" Washington asked, indicating another leather chair.

"Thank you," Laurens said. He stood beside the indicated chair and waited for Washington to sit.

"Billy Lee, two teas, please," said Washington as he sat down once again.

Laurens sat as well, his back stiff.

"Yes, master." Billy stood and left the room.

"Relax, son. You're not a flagpole. Tell me, your wife and newborn daughter are well in London?"

"Yes, sir."

"Good. She'll meet her father soon."

"It is my greatest hope."

Washington nodded and smiled. "Of course. Now tell me why you are here."

Laurens leaned back in his chair and took a deep breath. He let it out slowly and propped his chin on two fingers. "General, you are aware of my beliefs on the issue of slavery?"

Washington briefly raised an eyebrow and then coughed, clearing his throat. "I am. Your letters make it very clear."

"You are also aware of the attacks by the Tory, John Butler, and his Rangers in the Mohawk Valley?"

Washington sighed. "Just so. His depredations are a thorn in my side. They destroy crops and supplies while my army starves and deserts. I have ordered General Sullivan to march north and crush them."

Washington paused, thinking. "What has this to do with your views on slavery?"

Billy Lee entered and handed a cup of tea to both men.

Laurens leaned forward, a gleam in his eye. "Perhaps you have heard of a company of freed slaves that fight with Butler? They are led by a Negro named Captain Dick."

"Yes, I've heard of…" A sudden smile came to Washington's lips. "Ah, I see. You admire this Captain Dick." Washington leaned back in his chair and shook his head. "My friend, I haven't the power to manumit any but my own slaves. Even Congress would face a storm of protests."

"You have influence in Congress. If you—"

"More enemies than friends there, I'm afraid," Washington interrupted with a scowl.

Laurens leaned forward even further, his eyes wide. "General, let me raise a company of freed slaves. They will fight for their freedom, if not for this new country of ours."

Washington stared at Laurens. He stood, walked to the window, his hands locked behind him, and watched the rain fall on his drenched troops. Laurens stood as well and waited, breathing heavily, sweat beading on his forehead from the heat of the nearby fireplace.

After a deep sigh, Washington turned and walked to the map table. He placed all five fingers of his right hand on it, leaning lightly, and looked up at Laurens.

"If we gave you your head, and freed all the slaves today, what do you think would become of them?"

"Why, they would be better off, sir."

"Would they? Would they indeed? You are young, and

you live in a world of ideals. My world is a world of practicality and realism."

Laurens frowned. "They are not mutually exclusive. Slavery is an abomination. It must end," he said forcefully. "Sir," he added.

Washington pointed a long finger at him, his face stern. "Do not mistake prudence for weakness of principle, John." Laurens bowed his head, dropping his gaze to his dirty boots. Washington sighed, then sat once again in his chair.

"Let me put it to you thus," Washington began. "There are some half a million Negro slaves in this country. If they are freed tomorrow, will you feed them all? Will you teach them a trade? Will you employ them? Will you give them shelter? Will you protect them from the hatred and prejudices they will face? I am no friend to slavery, but I am also no friend to anarchy. We don't have the luxury to be idealists. The Crown has freed any slave who will fight for them, and what has happened? They die by the thousands of smallpox and hunger in squalor near their camps. Congress will never free the slaves and, even if they would, we barely have the means to fight this war, let alone provide for hundreds of thousands of destitute freemen. It may be noble to contemplate, but it would be ruinous to attempt. Let us secure our rights and our freedom as a nation first, so that the ideals we fight for may follow for each individual regardless of their color as soon as humanly possible. We are men after all, not angels. Make no mistake, slavery is a war of conscience and right that we must face, a war that may tear us apart in the future. But one war at a time, John, one war at a time."

Laurens stared at Washington. Only now did he notice the exhaustion in the general's eyes and the crow's feet that spread from their corners that hadn't been there six months ago. He sat slowly in his chair, determined not yet to surrender.

"And if we lose this war because we refuse to face the second? There are many who call us hypocrites for demanding our rights and our freedom even as we deny them to so many among us."

Washington's eyes flashed. "I do not have the luxury to lose this war. More evil has been done in this world, and will be done in this world, in the name of utopian ideals than in all the cataclysms of nature combined. We fight to get as close as we can to the perfect, and must be grateful for the nearly perfect. To throw it all away because we are not satisfied is the provenance of petulant children, not men."

Laurens bowed his head. "Yes, your Excellency."

Washington snorted, and then chuckled. "Stop with the honorifics. We are fighting to end the whole idea of nobility. I will write to Congress and recommend your plan to raise a unit of freed slaves."

Laurens looked up, grinning, his eyes wide. "Thank you, sir!" He stood, saluted, and moved to the door.

"John?"

"General?" he asked, stopping.

Washington stood. "After this war is over, and if I still live, I will free my slaves. But my moral obligation is to not compound the evil by throwing them to the wolves."

"Do you agree, Billy Lee?" Laurens asked, turning to Washington's slave.

"Don't want to be thrown to no wolves. You listen to the general," said Billy Lee, polishing the tip of a boot.

Laurens smiled. "I understand."

"No, you don't," said Washington with a chuckle. "But you might one day. Godspeed, Colonel Laurens."

"And to you, General."

Chapter 13
Winter Secrets

Richard and Blue made their way down an old native trail that led through a tall forest of pine that was pockmarked in places with patches of swamp. The early evening sky glowed with an orange hue. Their chores at the Rangers' winter encampment having been completed, they'd moved out to scout for a new pathway to Lake Ontario.

The camp sat on the west bank of the Niagara River, south of the Great Lake. A string of small log cabins was cut out of the forest, clustered with a large barn to shelter horses and some livestock. They were already several miles from camp, and the trail became fainter the farther they went. It ended, they assumed, at the lake.

Richard wore his work pants and Ranger winter boots—beaver skin, lined with mink fur—a wool shirt and light wool coat. The temperature had been hovering above freezing for weeks, a welcome reprieve from January's bitter cold. It was so warm, in fact, he couldn't see his breath.

Blue followed several steps behind. He wore little except a pair of pants and boots, and a pair of long johns. He rarely wore a coat, even in the coldest weather. He wasn't carrying a musket as Richard was, but his axe, as always, was strapped securely to his back.

Recently, Richard had begun to smoke a pipe, which he held clamped between his teeth. He liked the taste of the cherry-infused tobacco, and it gave him something to do with his hands during the long periods of boredom winter imposed. Made of kiln-fired white clay, it had been given to him by Sergeant Caleb. He puffed on it now and watched tendrils of smoke circle his head and follow him as he walked. The air was strange; there was a stillness in the forest that unnerved him. It was mid-February and there was no snow on the ground, which was unheard of, or so the locals claimed. "Gonna get it soon, you just wait," they warned.

"I miss Steps," Blue said out of the blue. "You think he doin' okay?"

Richard glanced over his shoulder at him. "Yup. He's having himself a time, I reckon. Lots of pretty ladies to keep him warm in his corner of the longhouse."

Blue chuckled and nodded. Steps had left for his village when the Rangers retired to their current winter encampment. "I'll be back come spring," he'd promised. Captain Butler had allowed him to leave, despite complaints from other soldiers who would have been considered absent without leave if they had done the same. "We need Mohawk eyes and warriors," Butler had said. "He's part of their tribe now, and I consider him a Ranger emissary to the Iroquois Nation."

They continued walking in silence, Richard wrapped in his thoughts. As usual, he thought of Shenandoah. She'd become distant as of late, pulling back even further into her usual reticence. They hadn't made love in weeks, and he marked it up to their lack of privacy. When they did make love, it was animalistic, brutal. She wanted to feel the pain, he knew, and he wanted it as well. It was almost as if she was blaming him for their inaction, for the numbing routine of early darkness and bad food, day after day.

Each cabin had four bunks, and the two slept together

on one with a makeshift curtain pulled over it from the upper bunk for privacy, although it was hardly private. The bed above them was empty, originally assigned to Steps. Ben and Blue occupied the other two bunks across the cabin from them. Lou had a cabin to himself, and often used alcohol to entice various native women—who plied the camp as prostitutes—to keep him company during the night. Richard had agreed to the arrangement after Blue and Ben both privately told him they wouldn't abide living in the same cabin with Lou. The two cabins were offset a few hundred yards from the rest of the structures, which kept the Black soldiers segregated from the Whites.

There was a squishing sound as he walked. He looked down and saw the ground had become porous with water. The path was almost non-existent. He stopped and looked around. Blue came up beside him, surveyed their surroundings as well, and looked up at the sky, which had grown darker.

"Maybe we should head back?" Blue asked.

Standing still, Richard watched the wind nudge the treetops. They were in a cathedral of giant pines, the floor wet and mushy, covered with layers of needles and cones. Through the waving tips of the trees, he watched roiling, sable billows of clouds mixed with tendrils of pale cream that danced across the heavens like tallow boiling in a pot. The stars gleamed, brilliant and crisp as diamonds, through the spaces between the clouds and then winked out one by one. A shiver ran down his spine. The air was still and pregnant with something. A sense of dread, perhaps.

Blue scratched his stubbly chin. "I don't like this, Captain. I don't like this at all. Storm's coming."

Richard nodded and shivered again. "Let's head back." He could see his breath now, an ashy gray as he spoke. He took the pipe from his mouth and tapped the cherry to the ground, where it sizzled in the wet mulch, then tucked it into his pocket.

It was when he turned around that he realized they were lost. Somewhere behind him the trail resumed, he supposed. But which direction and how far back, he had no idea. He'd left his compass at the cabin, not expecting to wander from the path. He paused and cupped his chin, looking for any clue. He looked at Blue, who shook his head.

"Don't ask me. You the captain. I ain't been paying any attention, been dreaming of a soft bed full of whores," he said.

Richard chuckled.

The wind stopped. The forest grew quiet as a buried coffin. He moved to the nearest towering giant and put his hand against it. Nothing, no pulse of life like he could always feel when he pressed his palm to living bark. He sniffed the air; it was antiseptic and pure—no smell, not even a whiff of the overpowering pine scent of minutes ago.

He pressed his back against the tree and slid to a squatting position. Blue grunted and sat beside him on the moss-covered trunk of a fallen log.

"Gotta think."

He always had his compass and a map, he always felt oriented, if not certain of his place in the world. He repressed the urge to panic, removed the pistol from his coat pocket that he used as a lighter, tendered a drop of gunpowder, and struck the flint. He held a tiny piece of kindling to the brief, sizzling flame and then used it to relight his pipe. He pulled its sweetness into his throat and nostrils. Shadows turned to deep gloom.

If he made a poor choice and they headed in the wrong direction, they'd make things worse. So far as Richard knew, he and Blue were the only men out of the camp, and both Sergeant Caleb and Shenandoah knew their general whereabouts. They could wait it out, knowing that their absence would be noticed and a search party sent out. How soon that would be, however, was unknown.

They could simply light a fire, stay warm for the night, and wait for rescue first thing in the morning. Caleb would certainly chew their asses out, of course, but there didn't seem to be any other choice.

"We wait it out until they come for us. Start gathering firewood," Richard said.

Blue grunted. "Figured you'd say that." But he didn't move. Both men remained stationary. That was when he heard what sounded like a whisper behind his right ear. He jerked his head to look. It was just a wisp of wind.

Richard noticed a few snowflakes. He looked up. Like the hand of an angry god, obsidian clouds scudded across the stars remaining in the sky. One by one, the stars died.

Then the deluge of white began.

****

Shenandoah paced in front of the cabin's fireplace, whittling. She paused briefly as she felt a sudden chill, then tossed a few more logs on the fire.

There was a small table in the center of the one-room cabin with four chairs around it. Outside of that, there were no other furnishings. She moved to the table with an ember from the fire and lit the oil lantern, then walked to the one small window near her and Richard's bunk and glanced out. It was beginning to snow heavily. She thought of Richard and Blue, tensed for a second, then relaxed. Both were smart enough to already be on their way home.

She glanced across the room. Ben lay on his back in his upper bunk, one leg crossed over a knee, picking at his toes. She rolled her eyes. It drove her to distraction. She took a deep breath and sighed. He ignored her, even though she knew that he had heard her sigh as clear as day. She chuckled and shook her head.

I'm going insane.

Every tiny habit and tic of someone that previously was merely annoying, or not even noticed, was magnified into teeth-grinding dislike and loathing to her lately. The rest of the camp had alcohol and whores to distract them, to help them cling to sanity. She had, and wanted, neither.

She took a teapot heating in the fire, crossed to the table, and poured the steaming water over herbs she'd carefully placed in a tin cup—Queen Anne's lace seeds and black cohosh. She let it steep and cool for a bit. Bringing it to her lips, she tasted it—bitter and pungent. Taking a deep breath, she downed it completely, swallowing the seeds and repressing the urge to gag. She looked up. Ben stared back at her then looked away.

She crossed the room and took Ben's book that sat on the mantelpiece. Walking to the table, she slammed it down. Ben jumped and looked in her direction, a scowl on his face.

"Hey!" He sat up, and swung his legs over the side of his bunk.

Shenandoah raised an eyebrow and pointed at the book. "Teach me to read," she said, evenly and calmly.

He stared at her, his brow bunched in a frown. Then he laughed. She narrowed her eyes to slits. He stopped laughing and jumped off the bed. He walked toward her, both palms up.

"Now calm down, Madam. I wasn't laughing at you…"

"Oh?"

He stopped in front of her and considered. Returning to his bunk, he pulled out a flask from under his mattress, moved to a small cupboard, and took two cups out, then returned to the table. He motioned for her to sit.

"I have a secret to tell you, but I need a brace of rum, and I think it wouldn't hurt for you to give it a try yourself."

She frowned, then sat, folding her arms. He sat as well and poured a few inches of rum in each cup. Pushing one cup toward her, he raised his in a toast.

"Here's to cheating, stealing, fighting, and drinking. If you cheat, cheat death. If you steal, steal a heart. If you fight, fight for a brother or sister. If you drink, drink with me!"

She laughed, picked up her cup, tapped it to his, and took a small taste. It burned bittersweet. She wanted to spit it out, but swallowed it anyway. The warmth settled in her throat and stomach. Ben downed his in one gulp as the wind howled outside. She looked to the door, and put Richard and Blue out of her mind one more time. For now.

She opened the book and pointed at a random passage. "What does it say?"

He sighed and offered to pour her more rum. She nodded. He poured a full cup and then refilled his own.

"It tells you about life, about love, hate, and death," he said, then looked away as he drank from his cup. "It's the doorway to the whole vast, goddamned world." His eyes began to water.

Puzzled, she looked at the indecipherable, tiny black marks on the page. At last, she understood.

"You can't read," she said softly and put her hand on his. "That's your secret."

He turned back to look at her. His lip quivered, and he nodded.

"How do you manage to…" She leaned in.

He looked down at their hands. "My owner's husband was an actor in the theater. He'd practice different speeches from Shakespeare's plays at home almost every day. I have a perfect memory. I can remember everything as if it happened yesterday, every word. I learned to mimic his speech, his mannerism. I became an actor as well. An actor in real life."

"You're Blue's hero, you know." She frowned. "You must never tell him. He wants to read more than anything."

"You think I don't know?" A low sob escaped his lips.

She came around and hugged him. He hugged her back and then held her out at arm's length.

"Those herbs you took can make you very, very sick, you know," he said.

She looked away. "I know."

"No menses?" he asked.

She shook her head. "No."

"Then these are our secrets, always between us only." He smiled and released her. "May God keep you in His care, and may the menses return."

She stood up, brushing the corner of her eye. "He's got nothin' to do with it. Now get your coat and boots. Something has happened to Richard and Blue."

Ben composed himself, nodded, and did as she asked.

****

It was as if someone had opened a duck-down pillowcase directly over their heads—an avalanche of light, dusty flakes. The temperature suddenly went south with a vengeance. Night came and drowned the light. Richard and Blue were washed in the sable ink of the darkest night they had ever known.

Richard staggered to his feet, but kept the tree trunk pressed against his back.

"Blue!"

He heard a muffled cry nearby. The snow was killing any sound, but there was enough to guide him. He reached his arm out in the direction of the cry and felt fingers brush his wrist. They returned and grabbed his arm tightly. He pulled the giant toward him, and they hugged in the darkness.

There was now no question of returning to camp. *We will survive or die here*, he thought. It was difficult to breathe; it felt as if someone had shoved his face deep into a snowbank, even though he was standing up. Clinging flakes pressed into his nose and mouth as he tried to inhale. The two men hugged tightly to one another. His fingers and ears grew numb from the bitter cold.

"A fire?" Blue said close to his ear.

Richard shook his head. Even if they could find dry kindling, the heavy snow falling would kill any attempt at a fire before it started. The only other choice was to try to find their way back to camp. But that was hopeless in this whiteout. Besides, the light clothing they wore, already soaked and beginning to freeze on them, would kill them before they got very far.

Their only hope, he knew, was to build some kind of temporary shelter from the falling snow to give a new fire a chance to grow. His pistol-lighter might save their lives. If they could clear a small space on the ground and prop a few sticks up, he could use his coat as a miniature lean-to above to protect the flame. He had kindling in his tobacco pouch. Then, all they would need would be dry wood. Since Blue had his axe, the stump he had been sitting on would still be dry under the bark's wet surface. He could chop into it and then extract enough to get the fire going.

"Better think of somethin' pretty soon, Cap'n. I'm cold," said Blue, shivering.

There was a groan from above, a brief silence, and then a cracking and tearing sound. Richard knew exactly what it was. He pushed Blue away and twisted aside, but his feet slipped out from under him.

A giant limb, weighted by the snow, tumbled down and smashed into Richard's shoulder, pinning him to the ground. The pain pulled a deep, animal growl from his gut. Then it gradually subsided, and numbness washed over the left side of his body. He lay there, his face up toward the avalanche of snowfall, and closed his eyes. He tried to catch his breath but couldn't inhale. He gasped and wheezed.

His teeth chattered and his body shook. There was feeling beginning to return on his left side, but he almost wished it wasn't. The searing pain brought tears to his eyes. He tried to call out to Blue, but nothing came from his throat when he opened it wide.

He knew it was only a matter of time before his body started to shut down, to turn pieces of himself off, and he'd quietly die. He couldn't feel his hands any longer.

He rested like that for what seemed like hours, but was probably minutes. He couldn't be sure.

Breathe.

He shook his head a bit to clear the snow from his face.

Breathe.

He tried to turn a little to relieve the searing poker he imagined was being thrust into his shoulder. He listened to the quiet, to the terrifying silence. He couldn't turn his head to look for Blue.

He closed his eyes, and his mind drifted. He was in Africa so long ago, in his mother's arms. Her eyes were oval like almonds, her hair soft in his tiny fingers, and her breath was sweet. It was nighttime, and a bird sang—a nightingale, he later learned. There were no lions near, for his mother was fierce and they were frightened of her, he knew. She hummed a melody to him as the bird sang.

Be still my child. Be still my child. We are all a song, and the song is love.

He heard a rustling and opened his eyes. Blue stared back, his face only inches from Richard's nose. The snow had stopped completely. He realized it must be at least a foot deep. Blood poured down Blue's face from a deep gash in his forehead and bubbled from his breath where it gathered at the corners of his mouth.

Blue said something to him that he didn't understand. Richard shook his head, frustrated. He tried, but still he couldn't move. Blue's teeth chattered loudly as he patted Richard on the forehead, then moved away.

He struggled but was finally able to turn his head just enough to watch Blue, who crawled about three feet away to where the huge branch that pinned Richard curved and cleared the ground by several feet. Scooping his shoulder down, he shuffled on his knees until he was beneath the limb, took a deep breath, then slowly began to raise his body, with the limb across his wide back. Muscles along his shoulders and neck popped out like thick ropes. Richard heard a groan and creak from the giant branch, and Blue shuddered. Taking another deep breath, he redoubled his effort, his entire body shaking.

A loud cracking noise from the tree limb came as Blue straightened, and the pressure along Richard's back and flank released. Gathering all his strength, Richard rocked to the side and rolled several feet, his face buried into the snow. There was a last groan from Blue, then another crash as the branch smashed into the ground where Richard had once been.

He felt hands grasp him by the shoulders and roll him over. He half-screamed, half-choked from the pain. Blue hovered over him, wiping blood from his own face, and looked him over carefully.

"Nothing's broken. But this," he said, pointing to Richard's bulging shoulder, "gotta get popped back in."

Richard shook his head, but Blue lay down in the snow, perpendicular to him, braced one foot in Richard's armpit and the other at the base of his neck. He took Richard's wrist, which was between his legs, in his giant hands.

"Where you headed, Captain Dick?" he asked. Then he yanked.

There was a *pop*, accompanied by excruciating pain, and

then relief. The absence of pain was itself pleasure.

"Home," Richard managed to croak.

"Damn right," Blue replied, moving to collapse beside him, head next to head.

They stared up at the familiar stars and the glowing moon.

"How come the moon can grab your heart and squeeze it like a ripe Georgia peach?" Richard asked the sky.

He heard a sigh from Blue. "'Cause you want it to, I guess?"

"Sometimes I think the moon is a gift the darkness gives us so we don't go crazy." Once again, Richard felt the sensation of floating above the endless sky.

Blue placed his hand on Richard's shoulder. "But we already crazy. We just pretend we aren't so we don't squeeze our own hearts to death. The moon is us, and we keep forgetting it every morning when the sun comes up. Been good to know you, Richard," Blue said. It was the first time he'd used Richard's name and not Captain Dick.

"My real name is…Ashley," Blue admitted.

There was a moment of silence as Richard fought the urge to giggle.

"You tell anyone, and I'll—"

"Your secret dies with me, brother," Richard assured him. After a few moments, he asked, "Why'd you kill your master?"

"He was my father," Blue said. "He raped my mother."

Richard nodded and closed his eyes. "Been good to know you, too, Blue."

After a while, the cold felt as if it was receding, and it

was actually becoming comfortable. He knew that was a bad sign.

He opened his eyes and stared at the brilliant half-moon that illuminated the forest with silvery shadows. He wanted to sleep, to dream. He wasn't so sure he wasn't already dreaming, for the earth seemed hunkered down in a white pelage—all was brittle sheen on a fox ear trimmed by the wind's tin whistle.

A native Ojibwe warrior rode from the distance on a pawing, dapple-gray stallion. Great billows of steam came from the horse's flared nostrils, and its tail bobbed high behind it.

He recognized the warrior. It was Wawasum, a lone chief whose tribe had been slaughtered while he was away in peace talks with the French the previous year. Behind him, the horse trailed a travois—two long wooden poles with heavy canvas between them used to drag heavy loads across the ground. Thick pelts and furs filled the sled.

He dismounted and walked toward the two men. Both men stared at him, but neither had the strength to rise. He wore a wolf's silver coat, and his legs were thick, lined with bear fur. Beaver pelts swung from his belt as he walked. His face was wrinkled and copper-colored.

He looked Richard in the eye, pulled a long hunting knife from his hip, yanked open Richard's coat, placed it against his throat, and then began to cut away the frozen shirt. He leaned in close, placed his ear against Richard's naked chest and listened. He pulled back.

"You will live," he said.

He did the same with Blue, who struggled briefly, but then gave up and let the Chief listen to his chest. Wawasum stood and nodded.

"*Gichi Manidoo* likes both of you," he said, smiling.

Richard didn't know what the words meant. Wawasum picked him up, his arms under Richard's shoulders and laid him down among the furs. He lifted Blue, who stumbled on Wawasum's shoulder to the sled, and lay down facing Richard.

Wawasum covered them with more thick furs, then tied them down tightly to the travois. He mounted the horse and dragged the two shivering men through the forest.

The rest of the night was a delirious dream. Richard remembered arriving in the camp before daylight. Shenandoah had already organized a search party with Sergeant Caleb, and they were about to set out. At first, the soldiers had threatened Wawasum, assuming he had killed Richard and Blue. But as the story came out, and as a very alive Blue and Richard assured them that they hadn't been killed, the Rangers gave him money for his furs, and liquor for helping two of their own.

The company surgeon warmed both men beside roaring flames, then in hot water, and slowly brought their temperatures back to normal. Richard had suffered some frostbite damage on his right foot, but not enough to keep him from walking normally. Blue, on the other hand, had no damage at all except for a prominent, and permanent, gash on his forehead, much to the astonishment of the surgeon. Blue was delighted, certain it made him even scarier to look at. Everyone wholeheartedly agreed.

Shenandoah was sick for a while, vomiting everything she ate for two days, but it went away, and Richard chalked it up to influenza. She seemed happy and no longer so distant.

Chapter 14

Emptier of Chamber Pots

Richard came to a small cabin that had been commandeered by Captain Butler as a command center, while the rest of the Rangers lounged at a temporary camp in a nearby clearing. The leaves had begun to turn, and the sky was gray and dreary. He'd heard rumors that a large offensive was about to begin. It was near the end of a long season of small successful raids and excursions by Richard and his crew, as well as other small companies, but the Ranger main body had yet to fight in a large engagement.

As he stepped to the door of the cabin, Sergeant Caleb rounded the corner and came to an abrupt stop, facing him. The two men regarded each other through squinted eyes. Richard knocked on the door and a loud voice from inside commanded them to enter. Richard bowed slightly, allowing Caleb to enter first.

Captain Butler stood with his back to them, looking out a window, his hands clasped behind. On a stool beside him sat an Iroquois warrior, Chief Joseph Brant. Dressed in comfortable English clothing, he fiddled with a folded map in his lap. Richard estimated him to be in his early thirties. His face was light-skinned, and he appeared more scholarly than fierce.

Brant commanded a group of fighters called Brant's Volunteers, composed of many Iroquois and Seneca natives, and had aligned himself and his people with Great Britain. He'd risen as a native Chief mostly because of his connections to the English king and his British education. His English was excellent. Richard knew all this and surmised that Brant and his native fighters, who were camped nearby, would be part of the new mission.

"Private Richard Pierpoint reporting as ordered, sir." Richard snapped to attention.

Caleb glanced at Richard. "Sergeant Coles be here, too, Captain," he said with a slow drawl.

"Stand at your ease, gentlemen," Butler said, turning around. His eyes were puffy, as if he hadn't slept for several days, and his face was unshaven, unusual for the captain. "This is Chief Joseph Brant of the Iroquois nation."

Both men relaxed and nodded to the Chief, who nodded back. Butler walked to Chief Brant and held out his hand. The Chief handed him the map in his lap.

Butler unfolded it, spread it out on a small table, and motioned for the men to approach. Chief Brant rose and joined them.

"As you are aware, General Sullivan—sent by Washington and the Continental Congress—is marching to engage us with an estimated five thousand well-provisioned and well-armed men. Their orders are to destroy the Iroquois Nations and kill or scatter all Loyalist troops, including the King's Rangers." Butler regarded each man in turn.

Richard shook his head. "We barely number a thousand, not counting the Chief's warriors."

They all looked at Brant.

"Two hundred at most," Chief Brant said slowly. "Two hundred and fifty maybe, with straggler White men."

Sergeant Caleb grunted. "Thirteen hundred against five thousand? If we stand and fight here, we're buggered up the arse."

"Colorfully put, but accurate. Unfortunately, our orders are to stand and fight," said Butler, then pointed at the map. "We are deployed here along the ridge, with the Chemung River below. Our defensive posture is strong, and Sullivan will have to fight uphill. Our hope is that the terrain, and the fact we fight from a defensive posture, will give us a decisive victory."

A long silence followed as each man considered their plight.

Sergeant Caleb scratched his stubbly chin. "This is madness. Why do we have no choice? Who's bloody idea is this, a goddamn dolt's?"

Butler coughed uncomfortably.

"We fight here and now, or I will take our people far north and west," said Brant with a dark scowl. "You White men can fight amongst yourselves."

"Figured it was you," said Caleb. He and Brant straightened and bristled.

Butler glanced at Caleb, then took a deep breath. "Against the advice of others," Butler said to Richard, "my father, Colonel Butler, is making you a captain in His Majesty's Rangers."

"A captain?" asked Richard, frowning.

There was a snort from Caleb, and a scowl danced across his brow. "A bloody captain?"

"Among your troops, and as far as the public is concerned, Richard is a captain. As far as myself and all other members of the military command in private are concerned, he is still Private Pierpoint."

Caleb threw his hands in the air. "Am I to be an

honorary colonel, sir? With an honorary stipend, perhaps?" Caleb asked.

Butler chuckled then turned to Richard. "I'm assigning Sergeant Caleb to your company, Richard. Let me make this clear: you command your men, not Sergeant Caleb. In all matters pertaining to military operations, both tactical and strategic, you will yield to his vast experience and training. Is that understood?"

"Yes, sir."

Butler turned to Caleb. "Do you have any objections?"

Caleb looked Richard up and down. Turning back to Butler, he said, "You mean…Will I fight… with Negroes?"

Butler remained silent, an eyebrow raised.

Caleb scratched his chin and gave a deep sigh. "I ain't fought with them before. They been fighting off on their own. I expect they'll fight as poorly—" he glanced quickly once more at Richard, "And as well as any other men. And if they be less than other men, I'll know it soon enough. What I seen so far ain't been too shabby."

Butler nodded and seemed satisfied. "Very well. Now-"

"Permission to speak frankly, sir," said Caleb.

"Granted."

"Sir, there'll be two of us commanding. Splitting command is a recipe for bunging things up."

"I know the risks. My decision stands."

"Yessir," Caleb said, shaking his head.

"Very well. We expect Sullivan to attack at first light tomorrow. Get your men to turn in early."

****

At night, a large bonfire burned in the center of camp. Richard sat on a stump far back observing the main group, carousing and dancing about the fire. Shenandoah came up beside him and sat on the ground, her legs crossed.

"So you're a real captain now?" Shenandoah asked.

Richard watched Ben, Blue, and Lou with the other Rangers tossing logs into the fire and drinking drams of ale brought to camp by Chief Brant. Captain Butler had initially objected, but once the men saw the wagon with its kegs, they weren't about to be denied.

"Not really," he said, scooping up a handful of dirt and flinging it in front of him.

Steps walked out of the shadows and leaned on a large staff he'd carved for a walking stick. Lou followed behind him, carrying a dram of ale, and sat behind Richard. They watched the spectacle in the distance.

"Drinking the night before a long march, followed by a pitched battle?" She shook her head. "A bad omen. You're a captain. Maybe you need to put a stop to this."

Richard shook his head, grimacing. "Only in name, and only among us."

Steps rose and glared at Richard. "Then be a captain among us," he said pointedly, motioning toward Blue and Ben. He melted into the shadows thrown by a stand of blue spruce trees.

"Hell, let us have our fun, Captain," said Lou, finishing off his ale. "We aren't children who can be ordered to bed when the sun sets."

Richard picked up another fistful of sand, ignoring Lou.

He stood and scattered it in front of him as he walked toward the bonfire.

"Captain Dick. A song. We want a bawdy song, by God," yelled Blue as he saw Richard approaching.

A cry rose up among the men.

"A song. Captain Dick, a song!"

Blue knelt on one leg and motioned to Richard. Richard smiled, walked up and climbed on Blue's back, who stood easily in the light of the fire. Men approached from the darkness until there were several hundred, all chanting, "A bawdy song. Give us a damn song."

Richard raised and waved his arms. The crowd quieted.

"I know many a bawdy song, but I fear they're too lewd and lecherous for the tender ears of yellow daisies like you."

Catcalls, whistles and hoots broke out.

"All right, all right," Richard yelled. "I'll sing the damn song, but only on one condition. You douse this fire and go to your beds when I'm done. Tomorrow you march and fight as honorable men, as true Rangers and warriors."

Blue jumped up and down, shaking and rattling Richard's bones. The crowd quieted, Richard cleared his throat, and began to sing in what he thought was a tolerable tenor.

> *Don't look at me that way, stranger,*
> *I didn't shit in your seat.*
> *I just came down from the mountains*
> *With my balls all covered with sleet.*

Screams of pleasure and laughter echoed. Shenandoah stood at the edge of the crowd, her arms folded and an eyebrow raised, watching him.

> *I've been up in the Mohawk Valley,*
> *Me and my old pal, Blue,*
> *A-pimpin' for a whorehouse*
> *And a God damned good one too.*

> *It was there that I first strummed Nellie;*
> *She was the village belle.*
> *I was only a lowdown freeman mack*
> *But I loved that girl like hell.*

> *Then along came a slaver Whig,*
> *A bastard all gay and rich,*
> *And he stole away my Nellie,*
> *That stinking Sonofabitch!*

Cheers and more laughter. Blue held a full mug of ale up to Richard. He grabbed it and downed it, took a deep breath, and sang the last verse.

> *I'm just restin' my ass a moment,*
> *And then I'm on my way.*
> *I'll hunt the Whig runt that swiped my…*

Richard paused as the crowd yelled the crude last word, then finished.

> *If it takes till Judgment Day!*

Blue spun around, then knelt as the crowd replied with thunderous applause. Richard slid down from Blue's back as men began to douse the flames and move to their shelters and tents.

Shenandoah stood thirty feet away, a scowl on her face and her eyes narrowed. She clapped her hands slowly and shook her head. Richard swallowed once and walked toward her.

****

It was deep night. Shenandoah lay on her back beneath the low-hanging branches of a spruce tree. The needles were about six inches from her nose. Her back rested comfortably in a shallow depression, and she held her musket to her chest with her eyes closed, breathing deeply. The smell of pine was sweet, with just enough sharpness to be head-clearing. The coming march and then the planned attack in the morning had kept her awake.

As she did almost every night, she replayed in her mind the muscle movements that were needed to reload a musket while lying on her back. Then she repeated them, over and over, faster and faster.

She knew she was fast now, faster than even the veteran Rangers she'd watch reloading. Her muscles had their own memory burned into them, and she could use her mind to think of other things as they flexed, from fingertip to wrist to elbow, bicep, and shoulder.

She removed her powder horn from her hip and was about to pour the grains of shot down the muzzle and into the bore when she heard a nearby sound. She turned her head slightly to the left to look.

About twenty yards from her, two men crept carefully, as if trying not to step on anything that would make a noise. Their black, full-length coats and dark Monmouth caps made them difficult to see, but Shenandoah's vantage point threw their outlines into focus against the sky. Each carried a long knife or short sword. She thought she recognized them from earlier in the evening, skulking with the group Chief Brant had allowed into camp and that Steps had objected to.

She froze and held her breath, watching them carefully. They stopped at a fork in the path that led, in one direction, to Captain Butler's cabin, guarded now by a single sleeping sentry and, in the other direction, to her and Richard's tent and then, farther on, to the rest of their crew's lean-tos. The main body of the Rangers and braves were several hundred yards beyond, behind a berm of tourmaline and granite outcroppings.

They whispered briefly and then diverged, one headed to Butler's cabin and one to her and Richard's tent. She knew a scream would probably not wake many people, not after the alcohol-infused stupor from earlier that evening.

She loaded her musket silently, pouring the shot down the muzzle, then a cloth wad and ball, which she tamped down with the ramrod. She rolled onto her stomach, primed the pan with powder, pulled the cock, then sighted down the length with one eye closed to protect her night-vision, as Sergeant Caleb had instructed the men.

She wavered, left then right. Captain Butler or Richard. She had one shot. Even if she hit one, the other might have time to complete their mission. They were almost out of range. She made her choice and pulled the trigger.

****

The crash of a firing musket filled the tent. Richard jerked awake from a deep slumber. He sat up, took stock of the tent in the darkness. He made out the shape of his brown bag of belongings behind the bedroll. The long shadow of his own weapon menaced like an intruder. Shenandoah's bag of everything she owned was piled next to his. He looked next to him. Shenandoah wasn't there.

The thumping of fast, heavy steps approached, and he saw the black outline of a tall man. The man tore the tent flap open and crashed into the small space, barreling into Richard's chest. The smell of alcohol and sweat filled his nostrils.

Twisting sideways, a knife flashed in the man's hand as the entire tent fell down on top of them. The man smashed his left fist into Richard's jaw. Richard grabbed the wrist holding the knife with both hands. The tent fabric stretched taut across his face and tangled his legs. The man grunted something unintelligible as Richard slammed the arm with the knife into the ground. He could tell the man was also tangled in the tent by the way he struggled on top of him.

The tent whipped from his face and he looked directly in the man's yellowed eyes. Richard pulled his head back and then jerked it forward, smashing his forehead into the man's nose. The man screamed as spittle and blood sprayed into Richard's face.

The man opened his mouth wide and sank his teeth deep into Richard's right ear. He gasped. Pain shot like needles through the side of his head as he struggled to keep his grip on the knife-hand.

He tried to blink the blood away, and caught the image

of Shenandoah leaning over them, her face contorted and her knife raised above her head. She plunged it deep into the man's back, who released his bite on Richard's ear and screamed again, his body twisting and convulsing. She pulled it out and struck again. And again.

The man went quiet, a dead weight on Richard even as Shenandoah continued to strike.

"He's dead. He's dead," he repeated between each of her thrusts. "Shenandoah!" he yelled, as his voice cracked.

She stopped and blinked, as if an entirely different creature had attacked. Her chest, legs, arms, and face were splattered by blood. She panted as she and Richard locked eyes. She rolled off them, and Richard pushed the body to the side, his hands still gripping the corpse's wrist. At last he released it. His hands trembled. Leaning to the side, he vomited and spat, then shook his head to clear it.

Men's voices, alarmed, rose from every direction, several running toward the scene, carrying lanterns.

Richard stood shakily, picked up the long knife, and pulled his breeches on. Shenandoah stood as well and moved close to him, examining his body. She touched his ear, and he winced.

"Not gonna fall off, doesn't look like. You likely got an ear like a cauliflower for the rest of your life, though," she said. She hugged him closely, and he grunted. His ribs ached where the man had crashed into him.

"I'm fine," he said, as he caught his breath.

He looked past her and saw Sergeant Caleb with a lantern and a group of Rangers in their long-johns standing over a body on the path that led toward Captain Butler's cabin. The rest of Richard's crew ran up to him and Shenandoah.

"Everything is fine," he told them. He turned and walked toward the group of Rangers. Behind him, Shenandoah breathlessly explained to their crew what had happened. As he approached the second body, Captain Butler exited the cabin wearing only his boots and underwear.

The man lay on his stomach, a large, bloody hole in his back. In front of him on the ground was a short sword. Sergeant Caleb handed the lantern to Richard and then bent down. He pulled something from an inside pocket of the man's coat. It was a rolled scroll, which he unrolled. He handed it to Richard, who examined it under the lantern's yellow light—white parchment with a handwritten note in cursive.

"Here lies the body of Walter Butler," Richard read. "A fugitive from justice, a scoundrel, and a sycophant to a tyrannical king."

Captain Butler took the scroll from Richard and examined it.

"I am no sycophant, by God. I worship no living man. As for the rest of it, well…" Butler shrugged.

The men laughed.

Shenandoah ran up and handed another scroll to Richard.

"Found it on the other one," she said.

Richard offered it to Butler who demurred. "Read it out loud," Butler said. Richard unrolled it and read.

"Here lies the body of the craven slave, Richard Pierpoint, also known as Captain Dick, an Emptier of Chamber Pots." Richard's eyes widened as he realized who wrote it.

Captain Butler raised an eyebrow. "I take it we need to

discuss this," Butler said to Richard.

"Yessir," Richard replied. "I know where this came from."

"It has been reported to me that but for the brave actions of this lady," Captain Butler said, bowing slightly to Shenandoah, "we might both be dead, Captain Dick."

Richard glanced at Shenandoah, who looked down at her feet.

"That we might, Captain. That we might," Richard said.

****

Richard and Captain Butler sat on small wooden chairs beside a table in the cabin. A candle burned next to them. They both ate salted beef and dried biscuits and washed them down with a pungent tea. The first tendrils of morning light crept along the dewy grass just outside the open door. Beyond the grass was a large oak tree. The bodies of the two assassins swung from a tall branch by their heels, with the messages they had carried attached to their foreheads by wooden spikes.

"Well, nothing much we can do about this Prescott chap now. I'll be posting a guard every night with you," said Butler.

Richard shook his head. "Please don't, sir. My crew will handle things."

Butler shrugged. "Suit yourself." He leaned back and stretched his arms over his head, then pointed through the door at the swinging corpses.

"You think I shouldn't have allowed the men to do that? Give me your honest opinion, Richard."

"This is war. They were traitors and assassins." Richard

looked down at his bare feet and touched the side of his face where the assassin had landed his fist. It was swollen and ached.

"But?"

Looking back up, Richard stared in Butler's blue eyes. He shook his head and sighed. "Every decision in life has consequences. Sometimes the world is a graceful swan, and sometimes she's a riled lion. Who knows what the next moment will bring? We're just men, sir, doin' the best we can. I believe in you, Captain."

Captain Butler nodded and stood. Richard stood as well. They shook hands.

"Now go get dressed and wake your crew, Captain Dick. We've got a battle to fight and win."

Richard saluted, turned, and walked into the early morning light.

Chapter 15

The Battle of Newtown – 1779

Ojibwe bodies—men, women and children—lay across the ground in the village, twisted into grotesque poses of death. Body parts were scattered like rotting fruit below an apple tree. They stepped silently through the carnage, their lips pursed and eyes focused forward. Richard led Captain Butler, Sergeant Caleb, and the rest of the crew. The racket of firing muskets echoed through the trees. It was mid-morning, and the stench of opened entrails and congealed blood wafted in the air.

For three hours they had repelled wave after wave of advancing troops from Sullivan's army. Their ranks decimated, the Rangers had retreated over the far side of the mountain to regroup.

Now past the village, Richard's eyes stung from musket smoke, his legs shaky and unstable. Blood ran down his back from a wound caused by flying splinters. Shenandoah panted and coughed, holding her knees. Ben leaned against Blue, his chest heaving as spittle ran down from his mouth onto his chest. Blue's axe was no longer blue, but crimson with blood, and swung back and forth from his left hand. Lou sat with his back against a tree, holding his head.

The roar of canons echoed in the far distance. From farther up the trail, they heard the tramp of many feet coming in their direction. Richard motioned with his arm, and the men spread out, hiding behind trees. Captain Butler came up next to him and they knelt behind a fallen log. Plumes of black smoke rose in the sky behind them.

The noise of approaching men grew louder and the crew loaded and wearily raised their muskets. The sound of men speaking and cursing followed.

Captain Butler raised his hand. "Hold your fire! They're friendly."

A small horde of native warriors moved toward them through the brush, bloody and exhausted, carrying their dead. The crew lowered their weapons and watched as the men trudged past, ignoring Richard and his crew.

Butler stepped in front of one of the warriors, who clutched at a torn and mangled arm.

"What has happened?" Butler asked the warrior in Mohawk.

"General Sullivan," the brave looked at him through a swollen eye and answered, also in Mohawk. "The Six Nations have been destroyed."

"My men?"

"Defeated. They scatter."

The warrior pushed past him and now Rangers, their uniforms torn, their faces splotched with powder burns, could be seen approaching behind the natives. Among the stragglers, a single soldier rode a horse—Colonel Butler, his lower leg drenched in blood and a crude tourniquet wrapped around his thigh. Captain Butler ran toward his father, with Richard and the crew behind them.

"Colonel!" Captain Butler said, grabbing the horse's reigns.

The colonel bent over and coughed, then straightened himself.

"Captain. I need your help."

"Yes, Colonel."

"Deploy your men for a holding action," the colonel said, pointing at Richard and the crew. "My soldiers need time to reach safety. We will regroup and make our stand at West Canada Creek." He reached his hand out and the captain grasped it. "Son, peace talks have begun and we must have time for as many of our people as possible to escape north before the boundaries are redrawn."

"Yes, Colonel."

Colonel Butler nodded, then looked Richard in the eye with a faint smile. "Captain Dick, you and your crew are a brave people. I commend you and wish we had met in better times. You have my deepest respect, and always will. God be with you."

"Thank you, Colonel."

The colonel nodded and moved on with his battered troops. As they tramped forward in one direction, Captain Butler and Richard led the crew toward the approaching enemy forces. Soon the last of the defeated mob passed them by and they came to a small hill where the trail descended into a meadow.

Richard deployed his crew to the left and right, where they knelt behind stumps and wide trees. Continental troops appeared about a hundred yards distant and began to sweep forward across the meadow. Richard raised his hand and held it. The woods were silent except for the beat of a snare drum in the distance, keeping time for the marching men. Closer and closer they came, until Richard dropped his hand. In unison, his crew's muskets barked and kicked.

Men screamed and dropped to the ground. The others

wavered, not expecting to encounter a picket line, then turned and fled as Richard's crew reloaded again.

"Flanked! Flanked by Oneida!" Steps screamed from the far left. Richard jerked his head in that direction. Oneida warriors rushed toward their left flank with tomahawks raised.

Captain Butler and Richard, along with Sergeant Caleb, Blue, Ben, and Lou, ran toward Steps and Shenandoah. She thrust her bayonet into the chest of a warrior and then spun to the side as his tomahawk flew into the dirt where she had been standing.

Richard barely avoided a spinning tomahawk and plunged his bayonet into the shoulder of a warrior. As he pulled it out, he was knocked to the ground by a man from behind. The two grappled and rolled into a ravine to the sound of screams and grunts around him. He grabbed a nearby rock and smashed the man's head, then wrapped his hands around his neck and strangled him.

He staggered to his feet. Blue's axe whistled through the air and severed muscle and bone as blood sprayed. To his right, Captain Butler went down when a warrior smashed the back of his head with a tree limb as he grappled with another man.

Shenandoah straddled a warrior who was face down in the dirt, and plunged her knife repeatedly into his back, spattering her face with blood.

A *wump* came from behind, and Richard spun around to see Ben smash into a man. The two careened to the ground. Richard grabbed a nearby musket and shoved his bayonet into the back of the man on top of Ben. The man convulsed and fell to the side, revealing a knife buried deep in Ben's stomach, just under his rib cage.

Richard knelt on one knee beside Ben as the noise around them quieted. Blood streamed from Ben's chest and he yanked the knife out before Richard could stop him. The stream of blood became a torrent as Ben pressed his hand to the fountain, unbelief in his eyes.

Ben coughed. "Well, hell."

Richard tore a piece of sleeve from his uniform and pressed it against the wound. Ben's head fell back to the ground and his eyes fluttered shut. Richard felt the heat from Ben's blood soak through the sleeve onto his fist and down his leg.

He leaned in close as Ben struggled to get a whisper out. "Give Blue my book…"

"The son of a bitch can't read," Richard whispered close to Ben's ear. He thought he could detect a brief and subtle smile on Ben's lips.

Richard leaned even closer to listen for breath, but after a bit he shook his head, stood, and surveyed the scene.

Dead native warriors lay around them in silence. Shenandoah tended to a gash on the back of Captain Butler's head. Lou and Steps each knelt on one knee, shivering and breathing heavily, their eyes downcast.

Blue walked up, dropped his bloody axe, and knelt beside Ben. He whispered in Ben's ear, grabbed his shoulders and shook the lifeless body. He picked the body up and hugged it tightly to his chest. The others gathered around.

Blue stared at each of them, then tossed the body, which crunched into a pile of leaves. "God damn this rotten world," he said, and stalked away.

****

They stood around a crudely dug grave as the sun set. At the head of Ben's grave were his worn boots. Richard held his Shakespeare book. He opened it, flipped through a few pages, then quietly closed it.

"Don't seem like the right time for this. One day…"

He handed the book to Blue. "He wanted you to have this—the only possession in this world that meant something to him." Blue hefted it and placed it carefully in his knapsack.

Lou threw a handful of dirt on the grave. "You wanna know what freedom really means for us? There it is." He turned and walked away.

A great horned owl launched itself from the top of a pine tree and glided over their heads. Its shadow slid across Ben's grave, wide wings that seemed, in Richard's spinning mind, to call out for the calm repose of darkness and sleep.

Chapter 16
West Canada Creek, 1781

It was the darkest of nights below a moonless sky. What was left of Captain Butler's command rested on a hillside encampment under a vault of stars. Richard and his crew huddled on a rocky outcropping that overlooked a small valley with a wide but shallow creek running through it. General Sullivan and his army, along with a sizable contingent of Oneida warriors, encamped on the hillside directly across from them. Occasional musket fire pierced the deep quiet, first from the Rangers, then answered by Sullivan's troops. It had been going on for hours, seemingly random, into the night.

Captain Butler paced behind the lines, his figure only an outline against the sky to Richard and his crew, who knelt and squatted in the darkness. "Stop wasting powder," Butler grumbled. "If you can't see 'em, don't shoot."

Steps and Lou sat with their backs against opposite sides of the same tree, their heads sunk to their chests, their muskets across their laps. Richard could barely make out the shape of Blue's lonely form, kneeling beside a granite slab that pierced the hillside. Always in the past, Ben was at Blue's side—like two brothers, connected by some unseen umbilical cord. Tonight, the solitary and faint shadow of Blue's giant form tugged at Richard's heart. He sighed and looked to Shenandoah, who rested beside him, sharpening her knife.

"Can't believe he's gone," Richard said.

"Well, he is," she replied without looking up. He tried to see her face, but it was hidden in shadows. "We aren't getting any closer to home, are we?"

Richard frowned. "We're still alive. That's something."

She looked at him. Her eyes were red. "Is it?" She returned her whetstone to her knapsack and sheathed her knife, then stood. "Is it really, Captain Dick?" She shook her head and walked toward Blue. She sat down next to him and leaned against his shoulder.

Richard heard a rustle beside him and turned to look. Captain Butler dropped to one knee beside him, folded his arms across his other knee, and stared forward into the darkness and the enemy camp.

"Captain Butler," Richard acknowledged.

"Captain Dick. You got plenty of dry powder?"

"Yessir. We're fine."

Butler rubbed the bandage on the back of his head. "Glad to hear it. You'll need it."

They sat in silence for a while. "Will we attack in the morning, sir?" Richard asked.

Butler stared at him. "Attack? Good Lord, no. We'll be lucky to make it to Carleton Island alive."

"Retreat then."

Butler chuckled. "Consider it an advance to the west in great haste." The smile dropped from Butler's lips. "I need you and your squad to do something for me."

"Yessir." Richard lit his pipe and pulled the sweet smoke into his throat.

"Our main body needs to move quickly westward, and I want you to try to draw their scouts northward toward Niagara."

Richard drew another long puff and nodded. "A

decoy."

"I need time to get our men, our wounded, and the Black men, women, and children, all the slaves you've freed so far, out of here."

Richard didn't hesitate. "We'll do it."

Butler took a deep breath and placed his hand on Richard's shoulder. "Make a lot of noise and leave a prominent trail, but don't let them catch you."

"Ain't caught us yet, sir."

"No, they haven't. Cross the Niagara River into the Ontario Provinces as soon as you can. The Crown is preparing homesteads for you and your people there."

"We'll fight another day!"

Butler shook his head and stood. Richard rose as well. "I'm afraid we won't, Richard. This war is lost. Do you understand?"

Richard arched his eyebrows. "What does that mean for us?"

"It means none of us can go home again."

Richard tapped the glowing cherry from his pipe, and ground it into the dirt with his heel. "That I understand."

Butler looked up at the stars. "We're all orphans now, Captain Dick," he said wistfully. More seriously, he added, "General Cornwallis has surrendered at Yorktown and the Crown is negotiating a peace. When that borderline is drawn, you and your squad cannot be south of it."

"Understood."

Butler turned to go, then turned back and offered Richard his hand. Richard climbed to his feet and the two men shook.

"It's a damn sight easier to start a fight than it is to finish one," Butler mused.

"To let go and just start floating with the current?"

Butler stared at him intently and then nodded slowly. "Why, yes. Something like that. Good luck, Richard Pierpoint. Godspeed to you."

Richard was about to reply, but Butler turned his back, and was already fading into the gloom.

****

They stood beside the Black Creek, a shallow but wide river, in the pale morning light. Captain Butler, the main body of Rangers, and what was left of the Iroquois warriors, crossed the river and moved into the forest. Richard held his crew back, and they watched the small army of men blend with the distant trees.

Richard pointed northward, parallel to the river. "We go that way." They regarded him, puzzled.

"North? Just us?" asked Lou.

"Niagara," Richard said. As he spoke, musket fire broke out in the woods on the far side of the river. He motioned for them to follow, and they broke into a trot in single file behind him along the west bank of the river. To their right, and across the river, the firing rose to a crescendo with screams and howls that Richard and his crew knew well to be common with hand-to-hand combat. Richard fought the urge to take his crew toward the carnage, and continued his sprint north.

They rounded a small bend in the shallow river to the right, giving them a clear view down the river from where they came. A single man stumbled into the water about two hundred yards distant, his sword drawn, and faced a line of Continental soldiers, their muskets pointed at him.

It was Captain Butler. Richard stopped his crew and they watched. Shenandoah moved toward the river, but Richard grabbed her arm from behind.

"No," he said gruffly. "That's not our orders, or our fight." She glared at him and shook his hand from her arm, but she stayed and watched with the others, their eyes wide.

Butler turned toward them, and it seemed to Richard he saw them, but before Richard could call out Butler turned back toward the menacing troops.

"Shoot, and be damned!" he yelled at them, waving his sword.

Ten muskets fired simultaneously. Three musket balls hit his chest, and one smashed into the front of his skull. His body twisted and collapsed into the water. Blood curled and drifted in the current toward them, black against the coppery stones on the riverbed.

Richard leaped forward, but now his own crew grabbed him and held him back. He jerked against their hands and tried his best to fling them off, but collapsed on his knees, unable to take his eyes off his fallen captain.

An Oneida warrior jumped from the far bank in front of the soldiers and splashed through the water. He knelt beside Butler's corpse, drew a knife, and quickly scalped him. He removed the dead man's coat, and held his trophies high as he crossed back to the far side.

Richard struggled again, trying to break free, but he was weaker now. Finally, Shenandoah whispered something to Blue, who picked Richard up, tossed him easily over his left shoulder, and the crew moved quickly and quietly into the forest, leaving the river and its blood-soaked water behind.

Blue set Richard down and they made their way through a deep forest, then through empty flatlands and a swampy marsh, and came at last to the encampment where the former slaves waited for the Rangers that now would never come to guide them to safety. They gathered in a small crowd—men, women and children—around fifty or so, and stared at the exhausted crew in front of them. They carried what was left of their belongings in small sacks and hand-made baskets, a few with hand-drawn carts.

"Captain Dick," the cry came from the children when they recognized him, echoed after by the adults. "Captain Dick!"

An older man with white hair stepped from the crowd, a grin on his face. A bandage wrapped his head. It took a second, but Richard recognized him—Isaac Whiles, the vegetable vendor from Connecticut. The two men embraced.

Isaac held Richard out by his shoulders at arms' length. "Well, if it ain't Richard Pierpoint, pretending he's that famous bastard everyone's talking about, Captain Dick."

Richard grinned and pointed to Isaac's head. "Y'all look like you buggered an Irish whore and couldn't pay up."

"I beg your pardon, sir. I always pay up."

Richard clapped him on the shoulder "That you do. I'm gonna need your help, Isaac." He walked to a tree stump and stood on it, surveying the crowd that gathered close around him.

"You all know you're not going to paradise. And you're not going home," Richard said. The crowd went silent. He pointed at Isaac. "You have a long journey ahead of you, and this man will lead you."

Richard watched their upturned faces, all newly freed slaves. He saw himself in many of them, the man he was when he first escaped his chains, young and looking toward a new life of hope and freedom.

Richard held up his musket. "The White man's king gave us a chance, not because he wanted to, but because he had no choice. If we've learned nothing in our bondage, it's that a man who will own another man is a thousand times less than free himself."

Eyes wide, they nodded in affirmation. He could sense the adoration in those eyes, and it made him uncomfortable. He cleared his throat and took a deep breath.

"Come with us, Captain Dick!" shouted a voice from the crowd.

Richard shook his head. "I have one last wager to make. Win or lose this great war, our brothers and sisters, our sons and daughters, all whose bones are daily pounded into dust by the slavers' lash and club, deserve the only justice I can give—to stay and fight. I will buy you time to escape north, to Ontario and a new life. Go now, and find a new home, a new beginning."

He stepped down in silence. And then the cheering began. He felt the weariness in his bones, the weariness that seemed of late to follow him around like weights manacled to his ankles. He wanted to sleep, to drift off into a nothingness that promised an end to the aches of his body, the aches in his heart, to give in to the lion's fang and claw.

As the cheers rose to a crescendo, Shenandoah leaned in close and whispered in his ear. "They love you. And I love you, Richard Pierpoint." She ran her hand gently down his jaw. Her eyes gleamed and she pressed her body against his.

The words he'd rehearsed many times, but always feared to speak, came at last as easily as gentle rain on a summer day. "I love you, Shenandoah." He kissed her.

****

Richard and his crew stood on a rolling berm of red clover and jasmine. As the flowers' sweet fragrance wafted around them, they watched Isaac lead the group on their desperate trek to freedom, along a narrow path that disappeared into the forest. As the last of the pilgrims from slavery was out of sight, Richard turned and moved toward the enemy's advancing troops.

Chapter 17
The Gaynde Waits

He knew he was going to die.

No more than twenty-five feet away, the lion watched him closely, its tail twitching. Its body was pressed flat to the ground, hips slightly raised in a pouncing position. Akachi's skinny eight-year-old legs trembled. Their eyes met and the lion growled, lip curled to expose yellow fangs. A second eyelid swept across the beast's orange-brown iris. Akachi smelled putrefied flesh. Above them, the great gnarled limbs of the baobab tree blocked the sunlight.

He'd left his mother, Ebele, only ten minutes earlier and still carried the short practice-spear he'd used during the morning's training with the other boys. His father had given it to him before leaving and disappearing for the last time a year ago. The rumors in the village were that he and three others had been swept up by the White humans to be used for food.

Akachi shivered at the thought even as the lion crept a foot closer.

"Go and gather some tamarind pods, Akachi. But stay away from the baobabs," his mother had told him. "You know there is an old *gaynde*, no longer a breeding male, who likes the taste of little boys and who has eaten two from the nearby village. He likes the shade of the trees."

She had shooed him away with her skirts as she worked on a large basket she had been weaving for two days. "Go now. Don't tarry here and bother me until it's time for mid-day sleep."

He had hugged her legs, then grabbed a small sack and

his spear as an afterthought and bounded away.

He'd hefted the spear at shoulder height as he sprinted, and his bare feet slapped the dusty ground.

I am a great warrior, he had shouted to the giant sky, his blood running hot through his veins like boiling watermelon-seed oil. Curiosity and hubris had pulled him to the baobabs.

As the lion stepped even closer, Akachi was not so sure about being a warrior. He stepped back slowly, spear raised to throwing position. As the great beast settled and was about to leap at him, he flung the spear with all his strength. It pierced the lions' flank, and the animal screamed as it twisted violently about, trying to bite the weapon.

Akachi turned and ran through the stand of baobabs toward a lake he knew was on the other side. He looked behind him—the *gaynde* followed, having pulled the annoying stick from its side, its head low, gaining distance quickly. His heart thudded as the lake appeared ahead. He stumbled and fell to the ground. The roar from behind him was like the earth itself had been angered.

****

"Richard," Shenandoah said. She shook him. He felt her hands on his shoulders and he opened his eyes. It was nighttime and her face was tensed in a frown and close to his.

He took a deep breath. "I was dreaming."

She wiped the sweat from his brow and hugged him. He shivered. He could still feel the fear rip through his body.

She rocked him gently and sung under her breath. "Be still my child…"

He looked at her. "Where did you learn that?"

She smiled. "My mother."

They were stretched out on their bedrolls under the stars. A twig snapped and Richard jerked to a sitting position, eyes focused in the direction of the sound. Shenandoah already had her knife in her hand as Richard reached for his musket. They both stood.

A man sauntered from behind the trunk of a tree about twenty yards from them. It was Lou. He held both hands up and Richard and Shenandoah relaxed.

"Where have you been?" Richard asked.

Lou set his musket down and folded his arms. Shenandoah shook her head, sheathed her knife and disappeared into the darkness.

Blue and Steps walked up in their skivvies, bleary-eyed and stared at Lou, who was fully dressed. Lou sat down with his back to a tall pine tree, his face expressionless and he stared, sullenly, at the ground. He picked up a handful of small stones and tossed them, one at a time, toward Richard's feet.

"I had a meal and the company of a lady."

"The hell does that mean?" asked Blue.

"Means I spent what little coin I get paid in this shit outfit on a meal—pheasant and cod. And a little perfumed company. It was damned good."

Richard raised an eyebrow. "You went into town?"

Lou tossed a stone that went *plink* as it hit Richard's musket barrel.

"Where else?"

Shenandoah emerged from the shadows. "You went into town, knowing they're looking for us?"

Lou tossed a stone that hit Shenandoah on the thigh.

"What the hell do you know? You ain't even a real Ranger, just a little girl with a knife, pretending she's a man."

He looked at Richard and sneered. "Best get your lassie in line before I set her straight myself."

Richard walked to Lou, grabbed him by the collar, and yanked him to his feet. They stared in each other's eyes for a moment until Richard released him. It wasn't worth the trouble, he decided.

"Break camp," Richard called out after turning away. "We're moving out."

Lou brushed himself off and tossed the remaining stones over his shoulder as the rest packed up their things.

"Looks like nobody else here appreciates the finer things in life. All I hear every blasted day is 'Make camp, break camp, move out, form a picket, load, fire.' Damnation and hell."

He nodded in Richard's direction. "Y'all got someone purty to knock boots with every night. What about the rest of us? We just fodder for your White king's cannons. Captain Butler and his damn king lost this war. He ain't my king. Ain't your king. The people we been killing are fighting against the whole idea of kings. I kinda like that, truth be told."

Richard turned to Lou, his eyes flashing. "We're fighting for them Black folks trying to make it north, to give them a chance, not for any bloody king," he said.

He pointed at Lou. "You been nothing but a selfish son of a bitch since the day I met you. Sometimes I think you weren't born to no woman. Y'all came out of a rusty keyhole nailed to a donkey's ass." Blue giggled in the background. "What's wrong with you?" Richard continued.

Lou slung his pack, picked up his musket, then spat on

the ground. "There come a day I stop fighting for other people, White or Black, and I start taking care of Hallelujah. That day nigh, sure enough."

"That's fine. For now, you take orders. We're moving out."

****

In the dark just before sunrise, the crew rested on a small mountain peak. Richard stood at the lip of a tall cliff, arms folded, watching the sky. Lou walked up beside him and coughed. Richard ignored him.

"You right," Lou said, just loud enough for Richard to hear. Richard looked at him. Lou's brow was furrowed and he rubbed his forehead with the fingers of both hands. "Sometimes I think all them whippings broke something up here." He pointed to his temple and chuckled.

Richard shrugged. "We're all broken somewhere inside. Being a man means getting on with life through the broken stuff. Look where you at," Richard said, waving his arm across the wide horizon. "You're alive and free, Hallelujah. After all you been through—that took grit and mettle."

Lou considered and smiled slightly. "I reckon you're right." He offered Richard his hand. "I apologize, Captain."

The two men shook hands. After a bit, Lou squinted at something in the distance, then pointed. Richard stared where Lou pointed and could make out the faint and distant lights of a small farmhouse.

"Ain't that the Boyle homestead?" Lou asked. "Where we shot that farmer with the machete?"

"I believe you're right."

Shenandoah walked up and stood beside them. She squinted at the lights.

"There's folks there that we need to warn," Lou said, an urgency rising in his voice. He turned to look at Richard and Shenandoah. "They've a right to know we lost this war."

Richard frowned. "I dunno. We really don't have time to—"

"He's right," Shenandoah interrupted. "If they don't get out of New York and into Ontario, there's no telling what will happen to them."

Richard sighed. "That's damn risky. Sullivan's men ain't that far behind, and they're in a hog's rush to bag the lot of us."

Shenandoah put her hands on her hips and tilted her chin up. Richard recognized the defiant pose, and he winced.

"I'll warn 'em and catch back up with you. I move the fastest," she said with a tone that seemed to assume it had already been agreed to.

"I'll go with her," said Lou. He put his arm around Shenandoah's shoulder, who gently but firmly removed it.

Richard's eyes flashed at Lou. "The hell you will. I haven't agreed to nothing."

Shenandoah shrugged. "He can come with me."

Richard stepped forward until he was eye to eye and toe to toe with Shenandoah. They stared. She didn't flinch.

Richard shook his head and stepped back. "All right. We meet up again at daylight. Shouldn't take you more than a couple hours. There's a small lake north about five miles from here."

Shenandoah nodded. "I know which one." Lou grinned and slapped her shoulder. She raised an eyebrow and he quickly stepped away.

"Don't bung this up," Richard called to Lou, who raised his hand in acknowledgment.

Richard stepped closer to Shenandoah and held her shoulders. "This don't feel right. We shouldn't be splitting up now."

She kissed him. "We owe that woman Oralee, and her grandkids, a chance to make it out."

Richard frowned and nodded toward Lou in the distance. "Watch your back. Something's wrong."

Shenandoah cocked her head, then laughed. "I can handle him, Captain."

"I hope you're right, Shenandoah."

Chapter 18
Remember to Breathe

S henandoah led the way as they approached the Boyle farmhouse, her musket slung across her back. A pair of oil lamps illuminated the front foyer through the window. There was no movement inside. She stopped and held her hand up, listening.

"Problem?" asked Lou.

She frowned. "Why they burning lamps in the middle of the night?"

Lou shrugged. "Who knows? Let's go find out." He moved past her and toward the house, but she put her hand out to stop him.

"We go around the back," she said, pointing. "And keep your voice down."

Lou frowned and followed her. "Whatever you want, boss."

The rest of the house, including the back, was dark. Shenandoah knew the back door opened into the kitchen. She turned the knob and stepped inside, with Lou close behind. There were dirty dishes stacked by the sink, and a pot on the stove half full of stew. Fat flies circled above it. Pieces of bread were strewn around the floor next to a broken bowl of stew which had spilled its contents.

"Load your musket," she whispered. Lou quickly did as she asked. She knew Oralee wouldn't tolerate a mess like this. The house was dead silent.

A faint flicker of light came from the doorway about

ten feet from her. Lou followed, his barrel pointed down and slightly to the right. She pointed at the light and he nodded as she moved a few steps more and came to the doorframe on her left. Around the corner, a boy coughed and then a *creak*, like the runner on a rocking chair.

Shenandoah poised just near the doorway. Silence. "Oralee? That you?" She took a deep breath and, knife in hand, stepped around the corner and into the main room.

To the right, Oralee sat in an oak rocking chair. Elijah and Marcus, her two grandchildren, knelt on either side of her, with her arms over their shoulders. Shenandoah could tell immediately that they were terrified. Oralee stared back at her. Her eyes pleaded, her bottom lip quivering.

To the left, Lucius Prescott sat in a chair, smiling. Three men stood behind him with muskets pointed at Shenandoah.

"Hello, Shenandoah," Prescott said.

She heard a rustle behind her and sensed movement. As she turned to look at Lou, his musket stock smashed into the side of her head.

****

Shenandoah opened her eyes to sunlight streaming through a window, but the light was piercing and she squeezed them shut again. She sat on the floor in a corner of the room. Her hands were tied behind her and she was gagged. The side of her head throbbed, and she could feel blood in her ear. She tried to cough, but it came out as a gurgle. Taking a deep breath, she slowly opened her crusty eyes again. She didn't know how long she had been out, but the hue of the sunlight indicated it was mid to late morning.

Prescott appeared in her face on one knee, only a foot or so from her. He tilted his head and looked her over. With a damp cloth, he carefully wiped blood from the side of her head. She tried to pull away, but he just waited until she stopped struggling, and then began to dab with the rag again.

As Prescott wiped, she looked beyond him. Lou and the three men stood in the opposite corner, watching. Lou avoided her gaze and stared at his feet. Oralee and the children were nowhere to be seen.

"Good morning, my little nigger girl," Prescott said with a raspy voice. His eyes were bloodshot and yellowed. His breath stunk of rum and rotting meat. He chuckled and patted her cheek. She jerked her head away as he stood and faced the men.

"You told me I'd get all of them," Prescott said to Lou.

"You will. They'll come looking for us," Lou said, then finally glanced in Shenandoah's direction. "Well, looking for her."

Prescott nodded. "I believe that. So, you expect to be paid."

"I got her here. He'll come for her, guaranteed."

Shenandoah tried to stand, but fell back again on her behind. She twisted her wrists, but the bindings were tight and expertly tied. They cut into her skin. She looked around for her knife, then noticed it stuck in Prescott's belt. She closed her eyes again and took a deep breath, trying to calm herself. The room spun and nausea gripped her stomach. She knew the anger in her chest wasn't helpful.

Remember to breathe, her mother had told her once when Shenandoah had gotten so angry she'd nearly passed out.

Breath is life. It was such simple advice, yet profound at the same time. She took another deep breath.

One of the men laughed. "Spirited little filly."

She stared at Lou, who avoided her gaze. Hallelujah's betrayal was a shock. The betrayal itself wasn't—it was her own blindness to it, to all the signs. This wasn't the man she'd known, who had suffered the lash for her when she had run. For some reason, she had clung to that memory of him through everything they'd been through, like she now clung to the dream of freedom and of going home. Something felt like it was breaking inside of her.

"You got no idea how spirited," said Lou. He looked at Prescott and his eyes narrowed. "Pierpoint is who you want. You'll be letting her go as agreed."

"Of course," Prescott replied.

He nodded to one of his men. "Pay our Judas nigger here his thirty pieces of silver, and not a coin less."

The man pulled out a purse of coins from his inside coat pocket and tossed it to Lou.

Lou opened the purse and looked inside. As he did so, the man who had tossed him the purse pulled out a knife and lunged at him. Lou twisted away and grabbed Shadrach Boyle's old machete from the mantle over the fireplace, whipped his arm around the man from behind and pressed the machete blade firmly against the man's throat. The man froze, eyes wide.

For all her horror and disgust at Lou's betrayal, Shenandoah hoped that Lou would succeed, that he could win against all these bastards. Her stomach turned over at the conflicting emotions.

"Drop it," Lou said. He drew the machete blade lightly

an inch across the man's throat. Blood dripped down. The man dropped the knife. Prescott and the other two men hadn't moved. "Now we're gonna back out of here, and I'll be gone. Our business is over."

Prescott rubbed his stubbly chin with his hand. He smiled and motioned to his men to back off. They stepped back, opening a pathway to the door. Still keeping the machete tight against the man's throat, Lou slowly backed out and through the door. He shoved the man hard back into the room and bolted out and off the porch. The man stumbled forward, then grabbed his musket.

Prescott put his hand on the man's weapon and shook his head. "Let him go. Sullivan's men will be here on the morrow. They're rounding up escaped slaves like this jackanapes. He won't get far. Got what I want."

Prescott glanced at Shenandoah, then pulled a chair up to face the front door. He sat and crossed his legs. "Come and get her, Captain Dick."

"Be careful what you wish for," Shenandoah mumbled through the gag. Inside, everything she had fought for during the last three years—to be independent and no longer a helpless spectator to her own life and choices—felt like it was slipping away. The image of her mother tied to the ground flashed once more in her mind. A bitter, bile-laced phlegm rose in her throat.

****

It was late afternoon when Richard, Blue, and Steps, approached the Boyle homestead via the main road. They knelt behind some bushes about a hundred yards from the house. Richard studied the terrain carefully. He motioned to Steps and pointed. Steps nodded and moved off, crouching low to the ground, toward the back of the house.

They had waited at the agreed meeting place. As the minutes had passed and she and Lou had failed to arrive, Richard knew something was very wrong. He had cursed himself for allowing her to go.

Richard and Blue approached the front steps. Blue unlimbered his axe and held it tightly with both hands. Richard loaded his musket, then carefully tried the doorknob. It was locked. He stepped back and kicked it open with his boot-heel. It flew open and he entered the room, his musket at his shoulder and pointed forward. Blue followed him.

In the far corner of the room, Lucius Prescott sat in a high-back chair with Shenandoah facing in the same direction, on her knees between his legs. He gripped her hair in one hand, head tilted back, and he pressed Shenandoah's knife to her throat. She was gagged and her hands tied behind her.

Richard didn't flinch, even though his worst nightmare stared back at him. He held his musket pointed steadily at Prescott's forehead. Two hulking men to the left and right held their own muskets pointed at Richard and Blue, respectively. Near the hallway, Oralee and her two grandchildren sat on the floor. She clutched them tightly to her bosom.

All stood frozen for several moments.

I can kill this son of a bitch before he hurts her, Richard thought.

"Now, gentlemen," Prescott said to his two thugs. They swung their muskets around from Richard and pointed them at Shenandoah's midsection.

Prescott cleared his throat. "Now, you can shoot me,

and maybe I won't manage to cut her throat. Maybe." He yanked her head back sharply. She grunted. Richard flinched, and took a step closer to Prescott. "But they'll blow two holes clean through her. Drop your weapons and we can talk about our differences like civilized people."

Richard struggled to keep his composure, to keep his hand steady on the musket, his eyes focused, his mind clear. He knew he couldn't win this skirmish, because the only thing he cared about was Shenandoah. He'd beaten Prescott in the past, however, had humiliated him. *I can do it again*, he knew. He fought to keep his eyes on Prescott, to avoid looking into Shenandoah's eyes. He feared he'd fall apart.

He lowered the muzzle of his musket a few inches. Shenandoah's eye's flashed. Ignoring her, he set his weapon on the floor. He looked at Blue who still held his axe tightly. Richard motioned for him to comply. Blue's arms, muscles bulging, trembled, his face contorted. He let out his breath, shook his head, and set his axe beside Richard's musket. The two men swung their muskets back around toward Richard and Blue.

Shenandoah's body slumped.

"Now call your man out back, Prescott said.

Richard cupped his hands around his mouth and shouted. "Steps! Stand down and come inside."

After a moment, Steps entered the room, his musket lowered. The third of Prescott's men followed him, his own musket pointed at Steps' back. He stopped beside Richard and Blue, and set his musket on the floor next to the other weapons.

Prescott removed the knife from Shenandoah's throat and released her hair. Her head fell forward on her chest, her eyes closed.

"Finally. The famous outlaw, Captain Dick. You had a good run, boy."

"Untie her," Richard said, nodding toward Shenandoah.

Prescott set Shenandoah's knife on the mantle beside him. He leaned forward, took her face between his hands and kissed her on the top of her head.

"Don't think so. In fact, I think she likes being trussed up like a little shoat and under a White man's thumb. You could learn something from her."

Richard clenched his fists, and perspiration beaded on his forehead.

Prescott placed his hand on Shenandoah's forehead and carefully pulled her hair back. "I think it makes her all warm and moist, like a summer melon."

"You bastard!"

Prescott laughed. He released Shenandoah and reached into a burlap sack on the floor beside him. He pulled out a human scalp and held it up.

"Know who this belongs to? This, gentlemen, is the scalp of the famous traitor, Captain Butler. Your commander, am I right? My patron will be happy and generous to acquire this lovely souvenir."

Richard clenched his fists. His voice dripped acid. "What is it you want, Prescott?"

"Well, a large detachment of battle-hardened soldiers is on the way, even as we converse, to take you all to trial for treason. But I have a plan to conduct our own trial right on this very spot. After we have a little celebration, of course."

Prescott stood behind Shenandoah. He pulled his riding crop from his boot. *Slap, slap, slap!*

Richard sneered, and a dark cloud passed behind his eyes. "She was right, you know. I kept her from slitting your goddamn throat."

Prescott flinched. "How's that?"

"I should have listened to her, should have let her dump your blood on the dust long ago."

Prescott leaned his head back and laughed nervously. "Oralee! Bring us some of old Shadrach's libations!" To his men, he added, "Take them down for now."

Chapter 19

Shakespeare's Justice

R ichard, Blue, and Steps were shoved roughly down the steps of the root cellar. Richard stumbled up against the cool earthen wall. The door slammed shut and he could hear a chain run through the handle, and then the *click* of a padlock. Small slits in the door allowed a bit of sunlight to reach them. Cobwebs hung from the roof. As his eyes adjusted, he noticed a body on the floor and he stepped back reflexively.

It was an old man in long-johns, his throat cut.

Steps dropped to one knee beside him and examined the body. "He died not long ago, no more than a day."

"I remember him," Blue said, shaking his head. "Name's Venture. Poor old bastard."

Richard climbed the steps to the door and motioned for Blue to follow him. He put his shoulder against it and Blue did as well. Bracing themselves against the wooden framing, they pushed against the door as hard as they could. It was thick and solid.

"It's oak," said Blue. "Ain't gonna budge."

"Again," Richard said, ignoring him.

Together, they slammed their shoulders against it. Nothing.

Richard slid down the steps and sat on the floor, his back against the wall. Blue tried again, but the door failed to budge. He sighed and came down as well.

"What now?" asked Steps.

Richard clenched his fists and beat them against his

temples. Then he took a deep breath and released it. The frustration and rage retreated, but only a little, and only temporarily. "Only thing we can do. We wait for them to make a mistake. They will. Only a matter of time."

"I ever get my hands around that bastard Hallelujah's throat, I swear to Lord God Almighty…" said Blue.

"We don't know what happened," said Richard.

"The hell we don't. Traitor sold us out."

"Worry about him later. Keep your mind on our current affairs," Steps said. "We get too far ahead of ourselves, we'll never catch up."

"Don't tell me what to do, you gimp bastard. Black man who thinks he's a Red man is confused in the head."

Steps limped to Blue, who stood and faced him, both men chest to chest. "And when the whip sang, it gave a shit what color you were, did it?" asked Steps between clenched teeth. "I'm a man, not a goddamn color."

Blue's eyes widened and he drew his arm back. Steps braced himself, muscles tensing.

"That's enough o' that shit!" said Richard.

Both men turned to face Richard. "What shit?" asked Blue, a scowl on his face. "You mean like giving them our muskets, and my axe, without a goddamn fight?"

Richard took a deep breath, but didn't break eye contact with Blue. "Didn't have a choice, and you know it."

Blue ran his hands through his curly hair, then slumped down beside Richard. "I know. I'm sorry, Captain." He looked at Steps. "I'm sorry, brother."

Steps put a hand on each man's shoulder. "That's right. Now we be calm. Prescott ain't as smart as he thinks he is. And those men with him got less brains between them than a sack o' hammers. Our time will come, and we be ready."

****

The slant rays from the sun swept slowly across the cellar floor, and moved from afternoon white to evening orange, and now began to fade. A large orange and red snake crawled from beneath Venture's body, which no longer held attractive heat, and slithered into a hole in the wall.

Men's voices, liquor-slurred and mixed with whistles and obscenities, came from the house. Richard and the other two climbed the steps and pressed their faces to the thin slits between the boards of the door. Richard could see the house, lamps already burning. Then a woman's high-pitch scream pierced through the laughter.

"Please, master!" It was Oralee's voice. The terror in it was thick. "Master, please. Please! Tell them to stop."

With his eye pressed to the slit between door-boards, Richard watched two of Prescott's men exit the back door of the house, each dragging one of Oralee's grandchildren by the nape of the neck, a long rope with a noose in the other hand. The boys kicked and whimpered. The men came to a large elm tree, and they each tossed one end of their rope over a limb.

Richard leaned back and battered his fists against the door, which shook and shivered. He pressed his face to the door.

"Prescott! You goddamn bastard, don't do this!" he bellowed.

The men glanced in the direction of the cellar and laughed. One staggered a bit and the boy nearly got away, but he

185

managed to grab him by the waist and shove the noose around his neck. The other man did as well.

Oralee burst out the back door, screaming. She ran up to the men and dropped to her knees in front of them, pleading and holding her folded hands upward.

"Please don't do this. I beg you."

One of the men lifted his foot and kicked her in the face. She rolled backward, her legs in the air. Her head lolled to the side and blood poured out of her nose.

Richard, Blue and Steps redoubled their efforts to smash down the door, but it remained implacable as granite. Breathing heavily, his fists bloody, Richard paused and pressed his eye to the slits.

The men hoisted the two boys by the neck high into the air. They tied the ropes off around the tree's trunk, stumbled back, and watched. The boys gripped the ropes around their necks and struggled, kicking their feet and contorting their bodies. The men began a little dance, laughing and mocking the twisting boys.

Richard dug his fingernails into the oak door. One of them began to tear, to rip from its root. The blood ran down his palm. He wanted to run to the children, to hold them up in his arms, to do what the world refused to let him do. He banged his forehead against the implacable wall of the world, again and again.

After a while, the two children tired and went quiet. The men stopped dancing and stood below them in silence.

"Well, shit. That didn't last long," one of the men slurred.

"We got another one inside needs to dance, too,"

replied the other.

"Hell, he won't let us touch her."

"We'll see about that." They staggered to the porch and entered the house.

****

Oralee opened her eyes and sat up. She went to rub her cheek and found her jaw was twisted sideways and wouldn't close. It was shattered. As blood from her face pooled in her lap, she looked up at her dead grandchildren who swung from the tree. A deep and anguished sob erupted from her stomach. She looked at the chained cellar and heard men's voices calling from it. She shook her head and took a deep breath. The pain from her broken face was horrible. Tears streamed down and mixed with blood. Getting on her hands and knees, she pushed herself to stand. Nearly falling, she caught herself and placed one foot after the other and then half-stumbled, half weaved toward the house. She climbed the steps and went inside.

She passed through the kitchen, looked around the corner, and peered in the main room. Two men finished tying Shenandoah, face down, on a low table, her arms spread to each side. She was on her knees on the floor. They'd removed her shirt, leaving her naked from the waist up.

Prescott knelt on the other side of the table in front of her, a powder horn in one hand, and a knife in the other. Two of the men held Shenandoah's shoulders pinned to the table. The third man was passed out in the rocker, a whiskey bottle in his hand. Shenandoah twisted and grunted, the gag still in her mouth.

Oralee went to the corner and sat quietly.

Prescott set the knife and powder horn beside Shenandoah's face. He pressed his finger against her forehead. She stopped struggling and stared at him. He untied the gag in her mouth and patted her on the top of the head.

"See what running got you? You understand now?" Prescott asked her. When she didn't answer, he grabbed her by the hair and yanked her head back. "You listening to me, little girl?" He released her head, and she nodded. "That's better. Now tell me you understand."

She smiled, still staring in his eyes, and spat in his face. The spittle ran down his nose and over his lips. He licked it and shook his head. His pupils contracted into sharp black pinpricks against the whites of his eyes, and his face contorted into a grimace. He reached behind him, grabbed an iron poker beside the fireplace, stood next to her struggling body, and swung it with all his strength against the side of her leg with a dull thud.

She screamed and her body convulsed as Prescott stepped back.

"Don't break her, boss. Leave some for us," said one of the men holding Shenandoah down.

"Gonna mark what I own," Prescott mumbled. He grabbed the powder horn on the table beside Shenandoah. "Hold her down tight." The men pressed all their weight against her arms and shoulders, completely pinning her face down on the table.

Oralee stood and tried one last time. "Please, massah. Please let her go." Prescott shoved her away and she fell again. One of the men kicked her hard in the stomach. She doubled up and rolled toward the hallway door. She climbed to her feet, holding onto the door frame.

Prescott opened the powder horn and carefully poured a line of powder in the shape of a large letter "P" in the middle of Shenandoah's back.

Oralee turned, went through the kitchen and out the door. On the back porch, stacked in a pile, were Richard and his crew's confiscated weapons. She reached down and tried to pick up the large blue axe. It was heavy, very heavy. Her head spun, and her heart hurt, like someone were gripping it in their fist and crushing it to pulp. It hurt so bad, she wanted to cry out. With all her strength, she dragged the axe by its handle across the porch and down the steps.

Below her swinging grandchildren, below a cold white moon, she dragged, yanked, pulled the axe toward the cellar door. Twice she stumbled and fell. Twice she pushed herself to her feet. Her legs grew numb, as if blood had stopped flowing to them. She heard encouraging voices from the cellar, urging her on.

When she reached the cellar door, she dropped to her knees, propping herself up with the axe-handle. She closed her eyes and panted.

I can't do this.

Captain Dick's voice thundered from inside the cellar. "You can do this, Oralee!"

She glanced at her grandchildren and then looked to the sky. The stars became the smiling face of her daughter, Coffey.

"It's the roses!" yelled the Captain. "Do it for roses in our lives."

She gripped the axe-handle and pulled herself to her feet. Her hands trembled. With all her strength, she heaved the axe over her head and struck it against the lock on the chain.

Sparks flew, but the lock remained unbroken. Knowing it was all she had left, she tried one last time, a moan escaping her lips as she yanked the axe above her head. She swung it downward. *Clang.*

The lock broke and the chain slipped through the handles of the door. She collapsed on the ground as the door exploded open.

On her back, her heart beat one last time and stopped. There was a quiet that enveloped her as men flew out of the cellar, and the cool air became warm like a blanket.

"Help her," was all she managed to say to the men.

****

Blue took his axe gently from her hands. Steps knelt beside her and placed his hand to her chest and his ear to her lips. After a moment, he looked up at an anxious Richard and shook his head.

Richard nodded. "You did good, Oralee." Steps rose and the three men melted through the darkness toward the house.

Loaded musket in hand, Richard peered carefully around the hallway entrance and into the main room. Two men held Shenandoah down, and Prescott stood above her with Shenandoah's knife and a flint. Richard could see the gunpowder "P" on her back. A deep moan came from Shenandoah. The third man sat in the rocking chair, snoring.

Prescott held the flint close to Shenandoah's naked back and struck it with the blunt edge of the knife. A spark flew, and the powder ignited with a flash, searing the letter into her back. She screamed.

Richard bounded around the corner and into the room, musket at his shoulder. He fired, and a musket ball exploded into the brain of the man on the left holding Shenandoah. Blue entered behind Richard, and his axe wind-milled through the air and embedded itself deep in the back of the second man holding her, severing his spine and killing him instantly.

The man in the rocker woke and jumped to his feet. He ran through the hallway door behind Richard and Blue, and came face to face with a musket pointed at his groin. It was Steps.

"This is for Talise," Steps said and pulled the trigger. *Boom!* The man collapsed, holding his bloody crotch.

Prescott tossed Shenandoah's knife on the floor and backed up against the wall, his hands held above his head. Blue pulled his axe from the man's back and Richard reloaded his musket, watching Prescott the whole time.

Steps entered the room with a blanket, and helped Shenandoah sit back on the floor. He placed it around her shoulders. Her leg was soaked in blood. She stood, lunged for her knife on the floor, grabbed it, and then launched herself at Prescott. Richard wrapped his arms around her from behind and pulled her back, her good leg kicking in the air. He set her, carefully, in the rocking chair and placed the blanket again over her shoulders. She shivered, eyes downcast and suddenly submissive.

"A whole regiment is going to be here soon. Let me go now, and they'll go easy on you," Prescott said.

"So if she can't kill him, who gets to?" asked Steps casually, ignoring Prescott and reloading his musket.

Blue shrugged, swinging his axe in a circle. "Guess it up

to Captain. I sure as hell volunteer.

Richard scratched his chin in thought. "What would that Shakespeare bloke do?"

****

Gagged and his feet bound, Prescott knelt over a thick tree stump in the darkness. Richard's crew stood around him, including Shenandoah. She used a thick branch as a crutch and her knee was bandaged.

Blue handed his axe to Richard who took it, and walked to Prescott.

"Time to get emancipated from your earthly chains, Captain Prescott," he said quietly. Shenandoah stared at Prescott, unflinching. Her face was impassive and her eyes cold.

"Ain't we gonna torture the bastard a little? Have us some fun?" asked Blue, confused.

Richard hefted the axe and stared at it. "Where's it going to end? We become him and he wins. I won't do it, you all understand? I won't take my pleasures from that rotten bag. Look here…" he pointed at his eyes, "…and you tell me I'm right. Y'all go down that path, and it'll poison your heart. Tell me I'm right, or you walk away and never come back."

He stared at each, one at a time, as they nodded to him. Raising the axe high above him, he swung it down and chopped off Prescott's head. He stepped back as the head rolled a few feet and blood sprayed from the corpse. After a minute, he walked to the corpse and cleaned Blue's axe with the back of Prescott's shirt. He handed it back to Blue, who examined it and limbered it once again.

Chapter 20

Niagara

Richard, Shenandoah, Blue, and Steps stood in a second-floor parlor of the Boyle home. Richard set a lantern on a small table and spread out a map. He pointed.

"We're here. That's the Niagara River. Closest point to cross is right here. We need to move as quick as we can before we're cut off."

Shenandoah shook her head. "We got to bury Oralee and those poor boys."

"Won't be time," Blue called from the window and pointed. "Look."

They moved to the window and stared out. Several miles or so down the road a cloud of dust rising above the trees was illuminated by a group of hand-held torches. The sound of men's voices and barking dogs carried easily through the night air. They returned to the map.

"How do you plan on crossing the river?" Steps asked. "It's wide, deep, and damned cold. Ain't no bridges."

"Hadn't thought of that."

"There's a Six Nations village just upriver here," Steps said, pointing. "I know them. I'll go alone and get a canoe. I'll be waiting for you."

Richard nodded. "All right then. Let's move."

****

From a hill overlooking the Boyle homestead, they watched the first rays of morning light creep across the landscape, revealing militia who swarmed the property.

Steps motioned toward a fork in the road. "That way. Don't stop—they'll have good trackers."

Shenandoah took Steps by the shoulders. "You be safe, Steps-in-Holes," she said, and hugged him. He winced at the use of his full name, and grinned.

"Still not used to my name after all these years. Be safe as well, all of you. We'll meet again on the Niagara." He turned and half jogged, half limped into the woods.

They set off down the trail Steps had indicated, Richard leading, Shenandoah second, and Blue in the rear. Their pace was fast now, with Shenandoah swinging her bad leg in an arc and hopping onto her good leg with each step. How long she could keep up the pace remained to be seen.

****

For a day and a half, they traveled toward the American side of Niagara. They rarely stopped except for water and to relieve themselves. The pace was grueling for Richard, and he had no idea how Shenandoah managed to keep up.

They stopped, finally, at a creek in the early evening to rest. Consulting the map, Richard judged them to be only about five miles from the rendezvous point Steps had designated.

Shenandoah knelt at the brook and splashed water on her face. Her clothing was soaked with sweat. Richard noticed she had been stumbling the last few hours. It didn't slow them down, yet, but he was growing concerned that her energy was being spent concealing from them how bad the pain was in her knee, rather than asking to slow the pace a bit. Each time he had looked back at her, her face had been implacable, unreadable, stoic.

Blue lay on his back, arms extended, and fell immediately to sleep. Richard chuckled as Blue started to snore. He stopped chuckling when, between each snore, he heard dogs barking in the far, far distance. Shenandoah stood, her head tilted to the side.

"Time to go?" she asked Richard. He nodded and shook Blue awake.

"Rise and shine."

Blue sat up groggily and frowned. "Dreaming of yams smothered in molasses," he said. "I expect breakfast ain't ready yet?"

"Not yet. We got us some work to do first."

Blue heard the barking dogs in the distance and sighed.

"Tired of running everywhere we go. When the bloody hell are us Black folk gonna be able to just walk through life when we want to?" Blue grumbled. "I ain't chopping no more trees down and, one of these days, the only place I'm gonna be running to is the breakfast table."

Richard smiled. "Today ain't that day, brother. Let's go."

****

Shenandoah clung to Richard's shoulder as they pushed through tall reeds, the ground wet and soggy beneath their feet. Blue followed behind. Torches lit the sky and the howling was closer now. With each step, a chuff of air came from Shenandoah's mouth, and her face was twisted into a permanent grimace. Tears rolled down her cheeks. Each time Richard tried to slow down, she pushed them forward even harder.

They crashed through the last of the reeds and the River Niagara lay before them. Richard scanned the shoreline as Shenandoah and Blue tried to catch their breath.

The river was wide, and the current looked brutal to Richard—small eddies and whirlpools spun near the edge. About thirty yards away, near a bend, Steps stood beside a large canoe, waving his arms.

The baying of the dogs was so close Richard looked back at the reeds, expecting the hounds to explode into the clearing any second. He could actually see torch flames bobbing not far behind, and men's voices echoed across the river.

"Over here! Hurry!" Steps yelled.

They ran the last yards between them and the canoe, a growl coming from deep in Shenandoah's throat each time her bad leg slammed into the ground.

Richard and Shenandoah reached the canoe first. Steps helped her into the boat, where she collapsed on her face. The two men pushed it out so that it floated and held it securely as Blue came up, puffing like a bellows.

Two men in uniform carrying muskets broke through the reeds where the three had first pushed through. They pointed, cursed, and then broke into a trot toward the canoe.

A musket boomed and the shot whistled through the top of the reeds nearby.

Blue reached the canoe and tripped on a root under the waterline. He crashed into the side of the canoe and went down on his knees. Richard grabbed him under his arms and hefted with all his strength. Blue seized the side and pulled himself up and over the edge. The canoe tipped precariously as Shenandoah tried her best to steady it.

Richard motioned for Steps to get into the canoe next. Another musket shot kicked up a splash of water near the back of the canoe as more men poured into the distant clearing. Richard yanked off his boots and tossed them into the canoe.

Steps jumped in and Richard pushed hard against the front, but the weight of two men and Shenandoah pressed the canoe into the mud below. He heaved, his back legs braced wide apart, but to no avail. Blue and Steps scrambled to the stern of the canoe and jumped up and down, freeing the bow at last. The canoe shot out into the water, dragging Richard behind. He gripped a ridge along the curved front as his body floated in the icy water. Blue and Steps grabbed paddles and dug into the water as the canoe picked up speed.

Richard glanced over his shoulder. A soldier stopped about thirty yards away and aimed his musket. He fired, and the ball slammed into the back of Richard's shoulder. He screamed and nearly lost his grip. Pain shot through his back and down into his legs. Losing control of his right arm, which flopped into the water beside him, he clung to the canoe with the fingertips of his left hand.

The current pushed the boat forward and it shot downstream. The men followed along the shore, cursing and trying to keep up, but fell farther and farther behind.

Richard looked behind him. His blood spread across the top of the water like oil, then slowly sank into the depths. The canoe rocked. Steps set his paddle down, stood carefully and moved to the bow of the canoe, which was now the back. He leaned over with his hand extended toward Richard.

Steps' balance was precarious. He tipped to the left, but couldn't quite reach...

There was a *boom* from shore and a musket ball slammed into Steps' chest and exploded, spraying blood and viscera over Richard and the water. He tipped forward, his eyes meeting Richard's, slipped into the river, and disappeared below.

"No!" screamed Shenandoah.

Richard's fingertips ached and he felt them slip. He grimaced as more shots from the shore fell around them.

At last his fingers failed him, and the canoe slipped from his grasp. Shenandoah screamed again. He drifted behind the canoe. Shenandoah tried to push past Blue, who was still paddling forward, but he held her back.

"Go back! Back to him." she yelled.

Blue turned his head and looked back at Richard, who shook his head. *No!* Blue began paddling in reverse, trying to go back, while Shenandoah fumed and raged.

Richard tried to swim with one good arm, but it was hopeless. He couldn't even swim with two. Pain shot through his right side like a spike. He was barely able to keep his head above water, and the old fear and panic gripped his heart.

Bam! A ball slammed into the lip of the canoe, sending a spray of splinters into Blue's arm. He brushed it off as if were nothing and kept paddling as blood flowed over his hands. Richard managed to raise his head above the water and screamed as loudly as he could.

"Go, damn you!"

Blue nodded, at last, and changed course again, paddling forward. The canoe quickly left Richard floating far behind.

The canoe pulled away from Richard as they drifted from the men on shore, whose voices began to fade.

The last he saw of the canoe in the moonlight was Shenandoah, her arms braced on both sides at the back of the canoe, watching him, until it passed a bend in the river and disappeared.

His head bobbed below the water and he kicked his legs. He rose slightly, but immediately sank again below the surface. He thrashed the water with his good arm, his legs scissoring as fast as he could move them. Once more, he crested the surface, then settled again with his head below water.

He felt like his heart was about to explode. He kicked and swung his arm wildly, hoping by sheer energy to break the surface again. Muscles began to tire and feel like rubber. His chest ached and blood pounded in his ears.

His upturned face just managed to break the surface, and he took one deep breath, then sunk again. He continued to struggle, but weaker now, and hung suspended in the dark, cold waters. He closed his eyes, hope slipping away.

His mind flashed back to when he was five years old. Chased by a lion, he ran into the cool water of a large lake. He knew he'd wounded it. The bottom quickly fell out below him, as the lion paced back and forth along the shoreline. He kicked and flailed his skinny arms as best he could, but soon became exhausted. He didn't want to die.

He kept his eyes open under the water. The first stars of evening looked down on him, were laughing at him, he thought.

He saw his mother's face through the waters above, her hands reached down below his back and hips, and she raised him until he floated comfortably on the surface. He sputtered and coughed. "The lion, the lion…"

She murmured to him. "Shhhh. You're my little lion who fights the world. Shhhh."

His breathing calmed and his muscles relaxed. He closed his eyes. Stretched out on his back, her arms beneath him, he swayed with the waves. She leaned in close to his ear.

"Remember this lesson—when you tire on your long pilgrimage—when you think death is near—lie back and the sky will hold you. Look there…"

He opened his eyes and followed her pointing finger to the stars.

"You see? Open your arms, lie back, for the stars will never betray you—lie back and you will live."

He did as she bid, extending his arms and spreading his legs, every muscle relaxing, his breathing deep and regular. He barely noticed when her hands receded, when she disappeared and left him floating above the stars below.

****

His opened his eyes. Above him, the water's surface was several feet distant. He relaxed. Opening his arms, he lay spread-eagled facing the sky. His body rose little by little. He broke the surface with his face and chest. He gasped for air and floated with the current.

Above him, a canvas of stars blazed, brushed by the tips of tall pines on both sides of the river. All was silent except for his soft and rhythmic breath. To his left, a quarter-moon hung like the bow of a fiddle, pointing downstream.

Time passed, though he couldn't tell how much, nor could he be sure he hadn't slept like this, floating on his back. His shoulder felt numb, with occasional twinges of sharp pain, and some feeling came back into his hand. But it all seemed to be receding like the time he nearly froze to death. It felt—comfortable.

Light fog skimmed the river and painted the tall trees in an eerie glow. He closed his eyes and, after a few minutes—or maybe hours, or maybe days—he felt his head bump something gently. He heard the sound of footsteps and assumed he was dreaming, felt no urgency to open his eyes and look. Even more gratifying, he felt no need to breathe. Breathing seemed unnecessary. He felt like it was time to go somewhere, he was late…

Hands, strong hands, grasped his shoulders and pulled him up and onto dry land. At last, he opened his eyes. It was Blue. A few feet away, Shenandoah leaned against a tree, blood dripping from her knee.

Blue laid him on his side and slapped his back hard. Nothing but the distant sound, a slight discomfort.

As if from a great distance, down a long tunnel, Shenandoah knelt on one knee beside him, her face contorted in pain and panic. He couldn't understand why she was so upset. He was worried about her.

She took his face in her hands and whispered in his ear. He couldn't hear what she said.

Another violent *thump* in his back shook his whole body. Noise slammed into his head. It was shrill but familiar. *Shenandoah*. With a deep, retching spasm, his body convulsed and water sprayed from his nose and mouth. He twisted left and right, and tried to scream, for pain returned everywhere—shoulder, hips, lungs, legs, every inch tingled and throbbed.

He coughed again, and again. He drew in a gulp of air

deep down to his guts, and coughed some more. Shenandoah held his face and kissed it repeatedly, tears in her eyes.

They pulled his clothes off and, after they helped him sit up, pulled Blue's woolen shirt over him. They rubbed his legs and arms. His back felt warm, and when he reached around with his fingers, he could tell it was blood seeping into the shirt.

The canoe sat on the river's edge not too far distant.

"Which side?" he managed to ask with chattering teeth.

"Ontario," Shenandoah replied.

So they had made it. When he stood, Blue's shirt hung down nearly to his knees. He laughed and shook his head.

"That'd make a good dress. What you think, ma'am?" Blue asked Shenandoah with a wink.

"Hem needs to be below his knees, in my opinion."

Richard tried to walk, but collapsed to his knees. He finally managed to steady himself by leaning on Blue's left shoulder. Blue held Shenandoah with his right arm around her back and her arm over his shoulder. She could barely stand as well.

As the three limped down a pathway in the forest near the canoe, the morning mist lifted and the sun peeked over the treetops. Around a short bend in the path, Ontario's Fort Niagara appeared in the center of a wide field. The grass sparkled with what seemed to be littered diamonds.

They approached the fort, and the doors swung open. Soldiers exited with two stretchers, placed Richard and Shenandoah on them, and carried them toward the entrance. Blue trudged along behind like a work horse pulling a heavy dray.

It was a beautiful morning.

****

It was 1815, more than thirty years since the three of them had made it to freedom. Fort Mississauga stood on the mouth of the Niagara River, not far from where they had crossed so many years ago. Richard and Blue, with other Black soldiers, hauled timber and downed trees through a glade toward a new redoubt. Lines of gray cut through Blue's short beard, and the same gray sprouted at Richard's temples and back of his head.

Named the "War of 1812," they had fought for two years, and the fight against the American invasion was over for the most part. They had beat them back, and were getting ready to go home to Garafraxa, Ontario.

Trimming a large pine log with a saw, Richard winced, then grabbed his lower back. Blue stopped swinging his axe at the base of the log and shook his head, breathing heavily.

"We ain't spry no more, Captain," Blue said.

Richard laughed. "That's a fact."

They moved to a small depression and sat on two stumps. Glancing up, Richard watched wisps of clouds skip across the clear, azure sky. Blue poured water from a jug over his head and handed it to Richard, who took a swig from it, then poured water over his head as well. He ran his hands over his face.

Blue stared at the sky. "It's a beautiful day."

"Yup, I reckon it is."

Blue nodded and clapped him on the shoulder. "Remember the day the three of us made it to Fort Niagara? It reminds me of that time when Shenandoah—"

"Yes. A new beginning," interrupted Richard and looked away.

Blue paused and stared at him. He shook his head. "Sorry, Captain. I meant—"

"Pay it no heed, old comrade. Every new beginning begs to be remembered."

Blue reached in a knapsack beside him and pulled out a large, dog-eared book. Reverently, he opened it and examined a page at random.

"That's Ben's book," Richard said with a smile.

"The Shaker of Spears." Blue ruffled through the pages. "I guess now's the time."

Richard stared into Blue's shining eyes. "I guess so."

Blue placed his forefinger on the middle of a page and began to read. "Now go we in content to Liberty and…and…" He shook his head and winced. Leaning forward, he handed the book to Richard.

Richard took the book from Blue. "You've been practicing," he said. Blue nodded sheepishly, a slight grin forming at the corners of his mouth. Richard looked down at the book and found the passage Blue had been reading.

"Now go we in content to Liberty, and not to banishment."

Blue sighed and straightened his shoulders. He stood. Richard handed him Ben's book and Blue tucked it carefully back into his knapsack, which he slung over his shoulder. Taking the jug of water, he poured it into a red kerchief, then tied it around his head. He ran his hand gently over the smooth blue handle of his axe, lifted it, and held it out to Richard.

Richard stood and accepted the axe with both his

hands. He held it up and admired it. "One hell of an axe," he said.

"Take good care of her."

"I don't suppose there's anything I can say to change your mind."

"Don't suppose there is," said Blue.

"All right then. What you hope to find?"

A faraway look crept into Blue's eyes, which twinkled and sparkled in the sunlight. "The edge of the world, I reckon. Westward, when the trees stop, then I'll stop. Everywhere is home to someone who never had a home."

Richard nodded and reached out his hand. Blue took it and they embraced. Turning abruptly, Blue walked toward the edge of the forest. As he neared the tree line, he stopped, turned, and saluted.

"Captain!"

Richard straightened and returned the salute. In a blink, Blue was swallowed up by his beloved trees.

Richard dropped to one knee, opened his knapsack, and pulled out a piece of white birch-bark wrapped in soft leather. He unrolled it carefully. It was a charcoal drawing of Shenandoah. She stared ahead, eyes proud and filled with the love of life.

"What am I going to do now?" he asked her as he gently ran his finger over her brow. "I miss you, you know."

"Fool," she said. "Go home."

He chuckled. He rolled the portrait back up, tucked it safely in his knapsack, hefted the blue axe at his side, and walked into a new day.

Epilogue

Garafraxa Township, Ontario – 1821

I n his dream, the sound of baying hounds transformed into the barking of a lonesome dog. Richard's eyes popped open. His labored breathing slowly calmed as he looked around his small cabin to orient himself. Above the fireplace hung a large blue axe and, beside it, a charcoal drawing on birch-bark of a beautiful woman, the woman in his dream.

He sighed. Sitting up on the edge of his bed, he placed his feet on the floor and ran his hands through his white, curly hair. Today was the day—his seventy-seven years of age no longer seemed to weigh heavily upon him. A wry smile curled at the edges of his thin lips and spread to the wrinkles surrounding his shining, mahogany eyes. Steady now, he rose and began to wash his face in the chilly water from an oak bucket on the single table in the cabin. He shaved with a straight razor, then dressed himself.

His cabin behind him, he walked up a worn path to a road that led, in the distance, to a small village. Sunlight splashed onto his face as the tall jack pines and red oaks parted, causing him to squint. No longer the powerfully built man in his dream, he carried himself slowly but with dignity. The ragged, threadbare Ranger's uniform hung loosely on his frame.

He made his way toward the center of a village carved from a hilly landscape. Men, women, and children came out of their homes or stopped their morning chores and gathered behind him. They were mostly Black, but some of the town's White folk followed as well.

He walked through the village with his head held high, even though his uniform's sleeves were worn and his pants were cinched by a belt in which he'd recently had to punch more holes.

Three children ran into the street. "Captain!" they squealed.

He blinked. The arms of the youngest still had folds of baby fat, and he threw them around Richard's leg. Richard stopped short. The other children were quiet, and the oldest boy, whose clothes also dangled from his arms, slowly extended his hand, wide-eyed, to touch the captain's uniform sleeve.

The girl, whose two thick, black braids gleamed in the sunlight, frowned and yanked her younger brother's shoulder. "Don't," she said. She turned to Richard. "Sorry sir." She looked down.

Her name was Najwa, and usually she approached him with a smile. Not today. He softened his stance, smiled, and winked at them. "Big day," he said. To the older boy, whose name was Napoleon, he said, "You can touch it."

The boy placed his palm on the Captain's faded emerald coat sleeve, then stepped back. Richard nodded to them and continued up the dusty street.

A small courthouse sat near the center of the town. He walked to the door and looked behind him. The crowd of forty or so people gathered around, their eyes wide. He took a deep breath, opened the door, and stepped inside. Everyone pushed in quietly behind him.

Bright light through the tall windows of the courthouse illuminated rows of benches before a high dais upon which stood a judge's bench. A small writing table sat beside it. Richard walked down the center aisle and stopped. He removed his hat, placed his hands behind himself in parade rest. His back went rigid as he waited, and the crowd moved to the seats along the walls. After several minutes of silence, a door opened behind the judge's bench and the court clerk stepped out, surveyed the room, and nodded. Spindly and scrawny, he reminded Richard of a stork.

"Mr. Pierpoint?" the clerk asked. His law wig was manicured to perfection and sat perfectly on his high forehead, which gleamed.

Richard nodded.

"Very good. I'll let the judge know you're here. Please be seated." The clerk glanced at the full courtroom, rolled his eyes, and returned through the door.

Richard sat in the empty front pew, alone.

Judge Horace J. Orr exited the private chamber, trying to adjust his floppy wig, his robes in disarray. Heavy and ponderous like a bear, the judge lumbered forward, followed by the clerk. A fat nose, which appeared to have been dropped by a soup ladle, punctuated the judge's face. His complexion was saturated with splotches of orange, and bushy red eyebrows shot like wings from his forehead. Everyone in the courtroom stood. The clerk made his way to the writing table. The judge sat behind his bench, adjusted his spectacles, and stared at the full lines of pews, frowning.

"Sit. Sit," he ordered.

"Hear ye! Hear ye!" intoned the clerk. "Approach and be heard! The Right Honorable Horace J. Orr presiding—"

"All right, all right. Enough of that twaddle. Sit down, William."

William sat with practiced elegance, obviously trying to hide his annoyance at being interrupted. Judge Orr nodded. With pudgy fingers, he picked up a small stack of papers in front of him and began to glance through them. He sized up Richard.

"Master Richard Pierpoint, I presume?" he asked.

"Captain Dick," screamed a voice from the back of the room.

Richard smiled and nodded.

"Yes. Captain Dick. Just so," agreed the judge, smiling. "Now, Mr. Pier...Captain Dick...you do realize that this is all entirely unnecessary? I am merely relaying the decision of His Majesty in this matter," began Judge Orr, slumping back in his chair. "This could have been accomplished behind closed doors." He adjusted his drooping, frayed wig, which had begun to cover his left eye.

"Thank you, your Honor," replied Richard in a firm voice, standing. "I am most grateful, but I wanted everyone to hear."

"Very well. William, please read Captain Dick's petition to His Majesty."

Standing and producing the paper with a flourish, the clerk began to read in an affected, high-pitched voice.

"The Petition of Richard Pierpoint, now of the Village of Garafraxa, a Man of Color, and a Native of Africa. Most humbly showeth: That Your Excellency's Petitioner is a native of—"

"—is a native of Bondou in Africa," Richard interrupted in a powerful and resonant voice.

The clerk coughed and turned scarlet, a scowl on his face. The judge waved the clerk down patiently, who then slumped in his chair, defeated.

Richard began to recite his petition from memory. "That at the age of sixteen years I was made a prisoner and sold as a slave, that I was conveyed to America about the year 1760, and sold to a British officer named Pierpoint and, after his death, to a Captain Prescott of the Continental Army, that I served His Majesty during the American Revolutionary War in the Corp called Butler's Rangers. That His Majesty's Government be graciously pleased to grant me any relief, I wish it may be affording me the means to proceed to England and from thence to a Settlement near the Gambia or Senegal Rivers, from whence I can return in my latter years to Bondou."

"Thank you, Captain. May I say that your service to His Majesty and these colonies has been most commendable." Judge Orr picked up another piece of paper. "I have here the answer to your petition by His Majesty's government."

"Your Honor?"

"Yes?"

"With your Honor's permission, I would like to tell my story before that decision is given."

The judge raised a bushy eyebrow and scratched his chin. "I'm sorry, but we haven't the time to—"

"Let him speak," came from the crowd, mixed with a low grumble.

"Order, order! Yes, well, you understand that I have no power in this matter? I am merely a humble spokesman for His Majesty?"

"I understand," replied Richard.

The judge surveyed the room's occupants. They seemed determined, as did Richard. He glanced at his clerk, who raised an eyebrow, smirked, and folded his arms as if to say, *See? I told you.* The judge snorted.

"Oh, very well. Please proceed." The judge yanked his rug off his head, shook it out and jammed it back on, then rocked back in his chair.

Nodding, Richard squared his shoulders, planted his feet firmly, once again placed his hands at parade-rest behind him, and cleared his throat.

"I was born in Africa a free man. I was raised as a child to be a warrior, and I have fought my whole life. I fought against those who killed my family, took me prisoner, and sold me into slavery. I fought against that slavery. I fought for the king against the American revolutionaries, because he offered me my freedom and they offered me nothing but a lifetime of slavery."

Richard's voice echoed in the rafters of the courthouse. The morning sunlight that streamed through the high windows made the lint that floated in the air seem like fireflies. The memory danced at the edge of his brain, but the words he spoke came easily.

"It began in 1776 when the colonies declared their independence from the Crown…"

****

When he finished, it was early evening. The setting sun cast shadows across the courtroom. For hours as he told his story, Richard had stood before the judge's bench. Sweat beaded on his forehead. Behind him, the crowd had gathered in a circle around him with small children sitting on the floor and the adults leaning forward or sprawled on the benches, their heads propped on their hands.

Judge Orr leaned back in his chair, his wig on the desk, his robes open, and his hands clasped behind his head. He stared at Richard, as William passed through the crowd, offering cups of cool water.

As he finished his story, Richard staggered to the left but caught himself and wiped the sweat mixed with tears from his eyes. The clerk offered him a cup of water, which he accepted and drank in gulps. Realigning himself and taking a deep breath, he resumed his rigid stance, hands behind his back, and stared at the wall high behind the judge. The room was silent.

The clerk lit lanterns that hung periodically along the walls of the courtroom, and the darkness receded.

"Please have a seat, Captain Dick," said the judge.

"I prefer to stand, your Honor."

The judge nodded. "Thank you for that story, sir."

In a small but clear voice, Najwa called out, "Captain Dick?"

"Hush," her mother said, placing her hands on Najwa's shoulders.

"It's all right. Yes?" Richard asked.

"What happened to Miss Shenandoah?" the little girl asked, her eyes wide.

Richard nodded, composed himself, and drank more water.

"We settled on a small track of land here in Garafraxa. We were the first settlers in this community."

He knew it was time to finish the last part of the story, so he centered himself again as best he could. He coughed to clear his throat.

"After we made it to Fort Niagara, Shenandoah and I settled down and built a small homestead together, the very cabin you see standing today. Wasn't much to look at, but we worked hard. Things went good for a while and, best of all, we were free…"

****

On a sunny spring day, Richard dug with a spade near the base of a stump. Nearly a year had passed since they had crossed the Niagara. Behind him, a small timber-frame cabin built from white pine stood in a large clearing of stumps. A pile of fresh-cut timber lay near the cabin, and a well-pump protruded from the ground nearby. He set the spade down and picked up an axe near the large stump, placed a cut log on the top, and swung to split it lengthwise with a *thwack*.

Other homesteads were being built in the same area, mostly by slaves and their families that Richard and his crew had helped to free. They'd followed him and were building their lives with him at the center of a new community, a new village.

He tossed the two halves into a small pile of split wood. Shenandoah, wearing a long dress made of light blue cotton, exited the cabin with a large jug. She walked with a slight limp to the pump, primed it with a bit of water from the jug, then began to fill it. He straightened for a moment and watched her.

Her leg had healed, but the limp was permanent. She joked about it sometimes, comparing herself to Steps. They would laugh, but the muscles of her throat would tighten and her eyes would shine as if tears were forming. She always recovered herself. She always thought he couldn't notice.

With his forearm, he wiped sweat from his brow. He

was naked from the waist up, dressed in woolen breeches and his Ranger boots which, while heavily worn, still held together well. Shenandoah walked toward him and handed him the jug of water. She placed her hands on her hips and surveyed the landscape as he drank.

"Can't plant crops until you pull these stumps, you know," she said.

"Gonna get us a couple mules to help pull them."

"I see. Know anything about mules, do you?" She regarded him with a raised eyebrow.

Richard shrugged. "Nope. They're small horses, I reckon."

She laughed. "Well I know something about 'em. They aren't small horses, Captain Dick. And they can be even more stubborn than you."

"That a fact?"

"Uh huh. Best get to digging. We got plenty of firewood." She turned to go, but Richard grabbed the rear of her dress and pulled her back. She spun around, seized the jug from his hands, and poured it over his head. Sputtering, he wrestled her to the ground. She giggled and twisted as he tickled her in her ribcage. He stopped and kissed her long and hard, then pulled back, smiling.

"You trying to drown me, Private Shenandoah?"

"Not hard enough, apparently," she replied, wiping dirt from his face with the palm of her hand. Her other hand caressed the scar from the musket ball on the back of his shoulder.

"Man that can float can't be drowned," he said and winked.

She rolled her eyes and stood above him. "Well, quit your floating and get to pulling stumps."

"How about I sing you a song, instead?"

She shook her head. "I heard a hundred of your songs, and they're all little-boy naughty. Pull a few stumps and maybe after dinner you can sing me a song that a real man sings to a real woman. How does that sound?"

She turned and walked toward the cabin. As she entered, she paused at a small rose bush that was just beginning to bloom with red blossoms. They had planted it in honor of Oralee and her grandchildren. Her hand gently touched one of the roses.

He sighed, pulled himself up, and began to dig at the base of the stump once more.

****

Their one-room cabin was bathed in the orange glow from a small fireplace. Shenandoah sat propped up in bed, sharpening her knife as she did every night before they retired. She wore a white cotton bed gown and her head was wrapped in a traditional African cloth she called a *dhuku* that she said her mother always wore.

Richard sat at a table and unrolled a large piece of white birch-bark. He spread it in front of himself, placed a large stone on each corner to keep it flat, and picked up a piece of charcoal he'd retrieved from the fireplace. He stared at Shenandoah, who concentrated on her knife like she was meditating, unaware of his gaze. He glanced down at the white surface and carefully drew a line with the pointed edge of the charcoal. He squinted at the line, then sighed. He rose, took a candle from the mantelpiece, lit it, and set it on the table next to his drawing. When he looked up again, she stared back with a quizzical look on her face as if to say, *what mischief are you up to?*

He chuckled and drew another line.

****

Richard stooped to wash some dirty linens in a small stream that ran about fifty yards from the cabin. He sweated profusely in the mid-summer heat. Beating the towels on a large rock, he rewashed them and then wrung them out. As he walked back to the cabin, he shook his head. Few stumps had been dug up from the property, since he hadn't been able to afford the mules he had wanted. They lived on a meager government stipend he'd earned from the military, but it was barely enough to cover food and sundries.

As he came to the cabin door, he pinched the stem of a rose.

He walked in and looked to the bed where Shenandoah lay, her head propped on pillows. Her face was ashy, her eyes closed. He set the rose in a small cup of water and placed it on the nightstand beside her. He took a small damp cloth from the washed bundle, folded it, and placed it gently on her forehead. Her eyes fluttered open and she smiled at him. She turned to her side, and he gently lifted her nightshirt.

Her back, where Prescott had branded her, was covered in sores and pus-filled welts. He dabbed lightly with a wet cloth. She winced, but didn't pull away or make a sound.

Two weeks ago, he'd taken her on a borrowed horse to Fort York, to see the nearest doctor. He had looked her over and said the skin on her back had grown infected and the infection, he feared, had spread to her blood.

He offered to treat her with leeches and wood bark, but when Shenandoah declined the treatment, he sent them home with a small bottle of tincture of mercury. The application to her skin had been sheer torture, and they finally stopped the procedure when the wounds didn't seem to improve.

Taking Richard aside, the doctor had said, "Prepare her for the worst. There is little I can do, and the process as she deteriorates will be agony for her and for you."

After cleaning her wounds the best he could, he stood back and let her skin dry before he pulled her nightshirt down. Keeping it clean and dry was all he could do.

Her breathing was rapid and shallow. A low moan escaped her lips and Richard winced, feeling helpless. She turned her head to look at him, seemingly annoyed that he was hovering.

"I'm okay. Go do your chores. I'll be better tomorrow."

He knew she was lying. "I know you will," he lied to her in return.

He kissed her on the forehead, then turned and left the cabin. He paused at the window and watched her from the outside. Thinking she was alone, she leaned her body over the edge of the bed and pulled out the bedpan. After vomiting into it, her whole body convulsed several times. She carefully set the pan back and curled into a fetal position.

He walked to a stump, picked up his spade, and began to dig.

****

Richard paused at the cabin entrance and picked

another rose. Behind him, the maple and oak trees blazed in red and yellow colors. He entered and replaced the drooping rose in the cup beside their bed.

He sat at the table, putting the finishing touches on his charcoal portrait. He glanced up at Shenandoah. She lay slightly on her side, the covers pulled up tightly to her neck. Her breathing was rapid, shallow, and labored. Her face was taut, and her forehead beaded with sweat. He looked back at the birch-bark and carefully smudged a line out with the edge of his thumb, then blew gently on the portrait.

"Will you show me?" Shenandoah asked, her voice surprisingly strong. It startled Richard. He looked up and smiled. He moved to the bed with the charcoal drawing and lay down beside her. He showed it to her. She looked at it closely through squinting, red eyes.

"Pull it back a ways. My eyes ain't good anymore," she said, a tremble in her voice.

He held it out a little farther from her.

She stared for a bit, then chuckled. "You weren't looking at me, you were looking up at your stars again."

"You don't like it?"

"Course I do."

She coughed, deep and rattling. A tear fell down her cheek. Richard couldn't tell whether it was caused by his drawing or the pain she suffered.

"You'll feel better tomorrow," he said, rolling the bark back up.

She looked directly in his eyes. "The hell I will."

He sighed, put his arm under her neck, and snuggled closer to her. She turned her head slightly and rested it on his chest, her favorite way to fall asleep.

****

Richard exited the cabin carrying Shenandoah, who was wrapped in a blanket, her arms around his neck. The day's heat had receded and long shadows cast from tall trees fell on them. He walked with her up a narrow pathway that led to a small hill with a view of a river in the distance. He set her gently on the ground with her back to a great oak tree that grew alone at the peak of the hill. He sat down beside her and they watched the sun begin to set in the far distance across the sparkling river. Tendrils of orange and amber light bathed them in golden hues.

They watched for several minutes in silence.

"Tell me again what your mother told you," she whispered in his ear.

"She told me I was her little lion warrior. She said that when we get tired on our journey, when we think death is close, we should lie on our backs, open our arms, and look up. She said that the stars will always hold us. That we needn't be afraid of falling…"

She nodded and snuggled closer. "This is my home," she said.

He brushed a strand of hair from her face. Her eyes were open, taking in the last wisps of sunlight.

She went so calm and quiet that he couldn't even hear her breathing. He sat and watched with her as the sky turned purple, then black. He looked at her again. She stared ahead blankly as fireflies rose around them by the thousands, like stars in a young night sky.

Beautiful daughter of the stars…

His eyes wet, he hugged her body.

****

In total silence, and after nearly ten hours of standing, Richard finally sat down on the bench beside him, his shoulders slumped.

The judge coughed and then stood. He tossed the paper he was holding aside.

"I won't bother reading this. As you may have expected, the Crown has denied your petition to return to your homeland, Captain Dick. By God, I wish it were otherwise."

A grumble rose from the crowd, and Richard held up his hand. They quieted.

"Now, I may have no power in this matter, but I do have some powers," the judge said, slamming his fist on his desk. "You are a brave and honorable man, sir. This government owes you more than mere thanks. I am ordering that you be given two hundred acres of prime land in this province for your faithful service to His Majesty."

Richard stood shakily. "Thank you, your Honor. I am grateful for the gift. But in order to keep this land, I will need to clear it of timber, build a homestead, and I will need to plant it with crops or I will lose this land, isn't that correct?"

The judge sighed. "Yes. This is true."

"I am an old man, sir," Richard replied, his voice faltering.

A man stood up in the crowd. "I will clear this land."

A second man stood. "I will build his home."

Two brothers stood in the back. "We will plant and cultivate the fields."

The judge smiled at Richard. "You see? Where you once fought, Captain, others now follow. This is not Africa, but you do have a home here."

Richard nodded. This new world was where he had fought and where his friends had died, where Shenandoah was buried. He felt relieved, mostly, to let the little boy lion, who fought everybody and everything, at last recede into the far distance.

****

Outside the courthouse, each member of the crowd either shook his hand or hugged him before moving off toward their homes. After the last had said their good-byes, Richard turned and strolled down a road that led not to his cabin, but into the forest. He heard a man's voice behind him and he turned.

"Captain Dick."

A young man stood before him, and beside him was his wife who held a newborn swaddled child in her arms. Richard looked at the baby and a soft smile broke on his lips. He reached his hands out tentatively. "May I?"

She nodded, and handed her baby to him. His finger parted the cloth so that he could peek at the baby's face.

"A girl?" he asked.

"Yes," she said. Richard's smile deepened and his eyes glowed.

"You always fought, Captain. Maybe one more time?" the man pleaded. "There must be a way we can help you get home."

Richard looked at the man, then back at the baby. He

placed two fingers on the baby's forehead, and turned to the woman.

"Will you raise her to be a great warrior?"

The woman shook her head. "No, I ain't. She's gonna go to school, and be a teacher."

Richard nodded. "That's what I meant."

He handed the baby back to her mother. His slumped shoulders straightened and he looked up at the sky.

This is my home.

****

The man and his wife followed Richard's gaze. A sea of stars blazed bright and hard above them. Or was it below them? Growing dizzy, they finally broke the spell and looked down.

Richard was gone.

They turned and made their way home through lanterns and candles that winked at them through windows, below the vaulted heavens.

The mother sang a lullaby to her child as they walked, a song that her mother had sung to her.

Be still my child. Be still my child. We are all a song, and the song is love.

The End.

Afterword

This is primarily a work of fiction. While we know some things about the life of Richard Pierpoint, many of those facts are either murky or opaque. That is to say, many of the facts we have tell us little about who he was as a man, or the struggles that he faced, the courage that he mustered, the failures he overcame and the triumphs he celebrated which mark human life as poignant, and thus beautiful.

We know, for example, that an African American man named Richard Pierpoint lived between the approximate years of 1744 and 1844. He was born in Bondou, Senegal, and was enslaved and transported in a slave ship as a boy to the American Colonies. He escaped his bondage and joined a British military unit called Butler's Rangers, and he fought against the American Revolutionaries. He settled near Niagara in what is now Garafraxa Township, Ontario, among a group of other Black settlers. We also know that he fought again in the War of 1812 on behalf of the Crown, and that he died without any known heirs or relatives.

My intention was to take those paltry facts and breathe life into the man, to give him struggles, failures, triumphs, loves and foibles. It was to create a story, without contradicting the known facts of his life, that gives him room in the world to walk about and learn and love and fight and die, that makes him real to today's readers, if only for a short time and in the pages of this book. It's a story that's rarely been told in the pages of American history and text books. I'm committed to telling the best version of the story, the version that is truest to the essence or spirit of Richard Pierpoint and those like him, if not the most factually accurate.

This is not a biography. The genre it belongs to is biographical fiction, which itself has a long history and a wide spectrum of approaches to historical subjects and to historical truth—from Robert Graves's *I, Claudius*, to Irving Stone's *The Agony and the Ecstasy*, from E. L. Doctorow's *Ragtime* to Gore Vidal's *Lincoln*. What is "true" in the pages of their books and books like them, and what is "fiction," is sometimes blurred and often *must* be blurred in order to tell a story that satisfies the human heart and head, and transcends the merely mundane.

I offer this book as a creation of love for Richard, and those like him, both men and women, who threw off their shackles, and hoped and fought and died for a better life and a better world.

Finally, I should mention that this story was originally written as a feature screenplay some years ago, and recently adapted to the novel format. It was inspired and commissioned by the Canadian producer and filmmaker, Brian Carver. I'd like to thank him for introducing me to Richard and his times, for his careful attention to historical accuracy, and for his wise guidance and advice, which was invaluable. Any errors or mistakes in historical accuracy are entirely my own.

****

For further reading about the life of Richard Pierpoint, I'd recommend David and Peter Meyler's excellent and exhaustive, *A Stolen Life: Searching for Richard Pierpoint* (Midpoint Trade Books Inc; 1st Edition, 1999).

For more information on Butler's Rangers and Captain Walter Butler, I'd recommend *War Out of Niagara: Walter Butler and the Tory Rangers*, by Howard Swiggett (Columbia University Press, New York, 1933).

To learn more about the lives of Black slaves during the American Revolutionary War and their quest for freedom, Alan Gilbert's *Black Patriots and Loyalists: Fighting for Emancipation in the War for Independence* (University of Chicago Press, 2012) is essential reading. His chapter on Colonel John Laurens, the American soldier and Patriot who pressed for the recruitment and emancipation of slaves to fight for their freedom, is especially revealing and well-written.